Gulping's Recital

GULPING'S RECITAL

Russell Edson

Tough Poets Press
Arlington, Massachusetts

Contents

Circus X 9

Love 21

Alfred 28

Father and Son 36

Flower 48

Father 58

The Death of Flower..........................70

The Courtship...................................77

The Marriage 83

The Soldier 94

"The Race of Man in a Midnight of Bubbly Fish":
Russell Edson's Narrative Teratology
by Mark Tursi 113

For Frances

Circus X

Are you listening? I am talking now. I must tell you about my father. No. How it is to wake up. No. About father. About our similar careers as soldiers and lovers. I have texts of father in my pockets.

Oh, I shall most certainly talk about death. Also dreams. Miss Wimp. And Flower. The Gulpings...

So that someone, anyplace in this world knows that he is himself; none other than he! Awakes from the shouting of angels and the hum of animals thick packed in the earthly regions.

Celebration, was it? in the fire gardens of heaven...and, oh, that drumming of animal blood and the clicking teeth of fox...

Suddenly the sun rose like an octopus from the sea, hung red like a parasol of hell. Quick now, I said amid the scream of birds...

And the man was rising like a drowned man out of the sea. Rising out of himself. Out of the darkness of himself. The lung of the soul nearly bursting...

Also the invasion of the children of the fly.

Blackly death is coming. In Circus X it is coming. Bleakly, brutally it is coming.

It is coming into the fingers because it is coming into the fingers because it is coming into the fingers. (I'm going fast now.) It is falling like a rain on any city. Like a fine rain when Spring is upon the city. It is falling through all the living like a fine rain, like a sweet rain, like a Spring rain. (I'm gaining my stride.) It is putting out the heart. It is soothing fires in the heart.

It is falling between people like a Spring rain. Between people on the stairway talking it is falling. Between people in a bedroom bickering it is falling like a Spring rain. Between people it is failing. It is falling over Circus X.

Pa Flower at night. Whiskey and cigarettes. Mexican breakfast in Circus X. A creature pinioned under the night. Crazy with stars that swarm like lice through the eyes, blighting the mind with a crust of fire.

In a moongrey house the window falls to the floor on a ray of moon. An old man lights his corncob in a brass bed. Grey angels in girlish-body dance, smoke from the old man's corncob gathers. He is nodding from his brass bed, smiling a smile turned inward. And in the great stalls of the night black horses flick their tails, hunching their necks, snorting.

The creature threw itself through a midnight of ocean, drowning stars, old men, horses, rocking horses, Gulping's recital, the race of man in a midnight of bubbly fish. He belches.

I said goodbye to Houseman in Torportown, where small trees grow low in spirals like springs of timidity, their fruit pinched like shy tears. And the wind only flicked leaves there as if asking, self-consciously teasing instead of swaying the whole of the tree.

In the Springtime the land was slow to green. And it took many months for Spring really to come. And then before

Summer had come it was Fall.

The people were hardly different. A man with an overwhelming desire might kiss his wife, and then cease talking to her for twenty years for his indiscretion.

And it was hard to light a fire, for even fire there was loathe to burn in public.

If someone without thinking happened to say, good morning, the other would've had to consider carefully what was meant by good morning, and finally would've said nothing.

They found it hard even to look into a mirror.

It is very strange, because these people were very warm. But each felt that the others were not.

In Jumpingtown, where all the men jump, is where the women also jump, and where the children jump. Up and down they jump like rubber balls. Old people just bounce to hell.

Many people just say, oh, the devil with it, and continue bouncing. They had tested this: they had stopped bouncing and seen that they were not bouncing any more. Once was enough, and so they started to bounce again.

They jump in unison, so that when a stranger comes to town it is as if the stranger were bouncing and they were not. But soon the stranger learns to jump, and it is as if he were not.

In Jumpingtown, when I was a child, people then didn't bounce. They were always lying down, that was all the rage in Jumpingtown, which was then called Pronetown. People would be lying in the streets, on the sidewalks, in doorways. And they'd never get up, they'd roll to where they wanted to go. Everything was calm; was calm, then. Most people just basked in the sun all day, lying in the streets all night under the moon.

But as I grew up and got more excited everybody began to jump. Everybody began to jump like blood throbbing in your head, their feet coming down in one's head on hot sunbaked pavement, year after year. And they've never stopped bouncing; and good luck to them; they'll drive me mad.

Goodbye to Houseman. Yes, we are waving aside the old air with our hands and handkerchiefs.

A vague raindrop, or a tear? easily brushed away. Another one. Will it rain?

Who is leaving? After all, Houseman is only human. Why should I feel any loss?

Is he standing on the porch of a grey tumbled house, or on the back of a train like a politician? Is he moving, or is it I?

I shall never meet anyone who is more than human. This saddens me. I can walk down hill to the mice. But up hill I will meet only man.

I shall watch the sun many a time and then I shall lie down. I shall think for a time. Light is strange. A grey twilight with a flash of red like a joyous wound. Limbs of the tree naked and stiff, a lonely structure.

The kitchen sweet with kerosene. The continuous scent of coffee, year after year. Bacon fat. Cabbage boiling. Fat comfortable feet in slippers shuffling on old linoleum, cracked, worn to the floor near the stove, near the sink. Ma Fletcher with her doughy pink hands making pancakes.

Houseman likes crepe suzettes. Not hand-thick pancakes smothered in Log Cabin syrup, pancakes that smell of bacon fat.

Whatcha think I'm gonna fry 'em in, buttta?

And oily coffee, iridescent with purple and green. Heavy, like to rot the spoon.

Pa Flower upstairs on his brass bed lying in a whiskey dream.

You better call 'im, he ain't et for two whole days, goin' on the night of the third.

These pancakes is like blankets.

We havin' baked potatoes, big shot; pig feets and macaroni and raspberry roth ringaling, an' if you don't like it you can take yourself some shit out the latrine.

I want a T-bone steak, french fries, an' some of that grenadine stuff.

Pa Flower called me upstairs. I give ya a penny if ya treats me to a fifth of Johnny Walker.

Ma Fletcher saying, you better not buy none of that city poison. You can go uphill to Father Fulton's still an' ask him can't you buy some sneaky pete. You tell him Ma Fletcher makin' some French kinda thing and can't she have some to cook it with.

Everybody know, said Houseman, that Pa Flower drinks.

You mind now, you tell 'em I cookin' Frenchy tonight.

Sarah Sinly said, Sarah Sinly is Pa Flower's little girl. She seventeen an' already goin' out with Captain Cough. He give her a brassiere for her birthday.

Pa Flower told her, don't let him touch ya none, that ain't nice.

Why it ain't nice, pa? You think he have a right to touch his birthday present, that seem only fair...

Where you get that Sarah Sinly from? She ain't a Flower or a Fletcher, she her own self from some other part of town, said Ma Fletcher to Pa Flower.

She Marion Spotch's child, said Pa Flower, by Mary Wilson, that woman-man useta hang around by Ralph River's Indian store. We been married goin' on five years up Hicks creek by Justice Minny, you know him, he, and, God rest his soul, Jack Hiss, useta fish by Priggen's Wharf this side of Fifth Frather.

Oh, sure, she the Spotch child.

One day, however, it was night one winter morning, a fire brightly ablaze. Pa Flower, full of sneaky pete, teetering, tripped and fell into the fireplace; caught fire like gasoline; crackling.

There he go, his poor life burnin' outa him like he made outa pork.

Jets like blowtorches shooting from his nostrils and mouth, from the sneaky pete. It almost sounded as if he were sighing. After the hair and clothes were burnt off he began to smell good.

He mighty tender with all his flesh permeated with that sneaky pete. God forgive me, I bet he have a fine flavor.

And Ma Fletcher couldn't resist picking up a pinky finger that had popped off with delicious aroma.

By God, it have a taste like chicken a la king, or somepin near it.

Here, give me some, said Houseman.

Sarah Sinly said, you gonna eat pa, there won't be nothin' to bury. That ain't the way he done you.

Come on, child, stop mashin' your gums an' dig in before it get cold.

Houseman had Pa Flower's head on his plate and was slicing the cheeks. Ma Fletcher had the hands.

She said, it have a taste like pig feet, only like chicken iffen they had pig feets. It's real scrumptious.

I, myself, could not bear the thought of eating a man who had offered me a penny.

Even Sarah Sinly, she was eating the unmentionables.

Captain Cough came in and had a slice of calf.

Time drifted. We got used to not having Pa Flower around. Sarah Sinly got with child by Captain Cough, and so they were wed and moved up to Apple Brashanwool, up north of Havor's. We found Ma Fletcher dead one day, back of the house, gnawing on a pig's foot.

Then it was just Houseman and me; and then even we parted.

And now I awaken to the twilight of common sense; coffee and polite tiptoeing toes.

Do not raise the shades. Do not tiptoe about. I see you are making coffee in the kitchen; and I swear you are brewing your own death.

Stand where you are or I shall shoot you with my dream gun.

If you touch me...How dare you touch me! My dream-tissue vibrates. Butterflies trickle up out of Hell's black bung. Touch me, you are touching a corpse. I am in my own dark hallway where shadows flicker from the banisters. And I hear laughter mixed in the firelight. And soon I shall be joining them down below in my Dr. Denton's.

Certainty, certainty...Certainty!
My God, my angel, you hurt me, I can not fly so high...
My angel...
My angel...

Not to think. Exploded. Stilled. My *self* gone; I watch the entrance. I do not judge...I am tired.

In the entrance, one bird-of-passage. It flutters outward. Little bastard.

The sun is very bright in a room. That is this way. When... Then there is a stone. There is very nothing to do. Why is there something to do? There is a stone with a shadow. This room. A chair because the table to rest a spoon on. A wall because the sky ends at the wall to separate birds from here.

Where are we? Now I want to change the subject.

A faithful clock still thinks we're playing the game. Even the sun puts its light through an east window. Later it falls out of a west window.

Let me change the subject again. A stone is what is a stone? Continual creation?

A stone is a stone. A stone's throw from a stone I threw another stone at a stone. I did not!

Shall I change the subject?

Sky.
Earth.
Earth and sky.
Sky and earth.
I don't want to think about that.
Why?
I would not want to think, except I can't help it, because I cannot see myself doing it. It just happens; which is very personal. Even I am not allowed that intimacy.

The stone. This is a passage.

A stone is not always a stone. That would be too much even for a stone.

I saw a stone. At least I was there. Or was it only the stone?

I saw a stone. No, it did not look back! It didn't dare, it had no eyes. The hell with it. And it is this way...

To get us closer. In an actual house. But there is no actual house... Let us say, in an old house, where Mr. and Mrs. Mouse are covered with Mr. and Mrs. Louse, who take blood for their evening meal... The throbbing of mice through the walls. A grey bubbling as dry as dust. Their eyes, like black drops of ink, are

looking over the miniature relics; a dead spider, a piece of silk...
Like pink fingertips, the infant mice at suck...

It is most fun to come here and remember other places.
Someday, long ago, in fine weather, we up to the cool, through
dark of the mountain, when yesterday I wondered if it were
tomorrow that I should think of yesterday. I was thinking yesterday that tomorrow I would be thinking that yesterday I was
thinking I'd be thinking today of yesterday. And yet, yesterday
I wasn't thinking about anything except thinking of what I'd be
thinking today ...
...About yesterday when I thought about nothing... Sometimes
I go to Paris when I am young. Or to London; when it is August
it is very hot; it is not possible to find a cold soda when I am in
London...oh, long ago...
What was I thinking about? It was, what am I thinking? And
what was I thinking? Oh, yes, when I am grown up I wish to be
a child.

This house is a city of mice. The man-plague is back. Commerce stops. Which of course is only thievery. This was the
house of man!

Upstairs in the bedroom, in the tomb of the moth, a few wasps
also died, watching the world imprisoned behind a window.
The room is like a monster's nest. The refuse of heavenly battle.
Broken moths scattered like dead angels on a felt of dust. The
chewings of mice.
I look out from the window as the flying insects must have.
What am I thinking of? That I am an insect soon to be chewed
by the mice? No, I am thinking that how could I yesterday know
what I would be thinking today?

Where was I yesterday as I began thinking of today? I was here, thinking what I am thinking now. This is yesterday. Tomorrow I shall be thinking about what I was thinking today.

That's funny, tomorrow seems like yesterday. Or today is tomorrow. What day shall be tomorrow?... I could swear it was yesterday that I was thinking that tomorrow I shall be thinking about what I am thinking...

Why doesn't it rain?
Why should it?
The world needs a washing...

What did the flying insects see? I am not alone with only God as they were. I have a monster...

From this height humans are no bigger than insects. Except they are very proud insects. Their asses puffing like awful engines.

They say, how do you do? They bow. They run. They walk. They dress in a variety of stuffs. But what are they, but awful little food machines, their foul little assholes. with them wherever they go.

And so I looked into my monster's eyes.

The most respectable Sir and Madam walked out with their assholes smothered in linen and lace...

I looked into my monster's eyes; there my face blooms on slick jewels. I kneel on his lap and look...

That man there has just left a pile of dung. He has made a sugar hill of dung. Thirty years of defecation; a foul mountain of peas and carrots, of pigs and cows and chicken legs...

Why do you stare? What are you looking at?... Such a fine fellow, my monster, speechless, formless...

I see a crowd of people. A thousand pursed lips, putt-putt exhausts; shifting, murmuring, drifting, sighing...
A line of men by white porcelain, with yellow strings. And women nesting like chickens.
A great foul fellow with a gold chain hanging across his bulging digester, locked a door, pulled down his pants and began to read his newspaper...
I have been among them, drinking their liquor. They tried to treat me as a son and brother.
Suddenly I shall be able to think the best thought. I drown their scorn with my hidden worth. Suddenly the flood of my finest moment! It passes, unnoticed...
I cannot repeat the voice from heaven that whispered quietly through my lips.
I'm tired of all this.
I looked into the eyes of my host and saw my two faces looking back with calm appraisals.
What is it then?
I have diminished the face of my host. After nine months preparation he emerged. Twenty-five years later this is the face, his face. I am behind his face looking out at myself. I am contagious. I bloom like a pox over the world. I see myself with his eyes.
Have you ever seen such an ugly face? Ugly enough to stop any process toward beauty. Beauty is superfluous in a world where my face lives, like a white stone in a brook.

After all, they shall turn me out with politeness. I shall go tipsily, like an ancient king. My host sighs with relief. But he oughtn't to, because, though I'm a billion miles away, and always have been, still, I can feel that sigh. It ignites my humor. The best thing about him is his liquor; and other men made that!...

To illustrate what I'm getting at, let us talk of cheese. We must go back to Circus X.

In Circus X they say, please pass the cheese. And they keep saying it, because there is no cheese in this dear world.

They say, please, let me have just a tiny bit of cheese. But in this empty world there is not the slightest chance of anything.

Now if you like a stone, all the stones vanish.

Because *who* wants a stone, or a piece of cheese?...

In Circus X they say, please pass the cheese. They rattle their forks and knives. They drum with their feet.

Now if you wanted a stone might not all the stones vanish?

Impatience mounts. Where is the cheese? Shall we grow old waiting?

If a great wheel of cheese came to Circus X, they would still say, please pass the cheese. And while eating it, still they will say, please, I beg you, please, if you ever loved me, please, pass the cheese.

And long after the appetite is laid in the ground with Dr. Flower, still his ghost will come, saying, please pass the cheese.

And what is cheese? This is what it is, it is cheese because I want it. And after I have my cheese, I want it. Because I can not have it, even if I do.

So like a woman is cheese...

Love

Why talk of cheese when one can talk of women? Or of women when one can talk of mother? I do not know.

Let us get on.

Love is how we go wrong. We only live because we have no love. Love is the need to die. Yes, so let us talk about death.

First, a background placed in August, the month of anguish...

Love is long ago. It is in August, an August that has no year. As if August were a room...

If I see the slight hint of mirth suppressing itself by your mouth, I shall vomit.

Love is a very long time ago... Yes, that's it. Love is a very long time ago, exactly the words in the garden. So surely is it as death is. As are the blue eggs of the robin. As is the red shadow of the rose at twilight... Is as surely as time or the garden, so very long ago.

What we did, for we are laughing again. Though the waters waver in the empty cave of then; what we did, for we are laughing, so surely in the August twilight; the weather was pink; *what we will do tomorrow when the snow thaws.*

You will remember the unearthly smell of earth when Spring shocked the quiet world. The tender explosion of forsythia...

So surely as the bundle of letters wrapped in blue string in the drawer of the writing-table by the north window of the room;

so exactly the words so long ago in the garden.

And you will remember because we are again the laughter, as if tomorrow when the snow thaws...

Laughter one August twilight. You can hear the hot cry of a distant train. The sheets are cool. I see you faintly. The dark between your thighs. Your head is back.

You will remember coffee and cigarettes and roses growing in vine on the windowsill. In the morning, sunshine; ice-fire on the ocean. Our year was new. August, when a dog is barking, and what we read in the newspaper...

A thin moon and the late month.

It is, you will remember as you remember tomorrow, when the snow thaws, the desire in the hot weathers of infinite August. Tomorrow, when the snow thaws.

And you will remember love is a very long time ago, exactly the words in the garden...

Here, I think I have a love-letter. It may be to my father. Does it matter?

When love is dead... Or is it mine? Does it matter? I don't remember... It may be...although I don't think anyone ever...

If this turns out to be a business letter, stop me, because I'm quite sure it'll be none of your business.

So many papers. Texts of father's, darling scraps of paper that I've kept through the years, using one now and again in lieu of a handkerchief or a toilet tissue, even as a white flag in times of shame; sperm-catchers.

But the letter: Dear Larry, I am so sorry you are fighting the Hun. But you must bear up for my sake. It is not easy sitting by the window watching the moon and wondering what it will see when it comes to where you are.

Sometimes I wake in the night, for I see your beautiful body full of infant flies.

Last midnight the sun was very bright and I saw you bleeding in the grass.

Aunt Peelya said I must bear up for your sake. Mr. Meat says that if I don't get hold of myself I shall become a *bad girl.*

But your body is full of bullets, and your penis cold and insufficient.

I told Mr. Meat to mind Mrs. Meat.

Larry, do you mind that I play a game called *Larry?* I play it with any man who's willing to play. They think I'm an *easy one.* Oh, she's easy, they say. Oh, you would giggle if you could see it. They are such fools; they are not at all like you, Larry, my beautiful one.

I transform them, I make them into *Larry.* When I say, I love you, it is *you* I love, not them. They are so ardent, but it is really you I love.

I told Aunt Peelya that you said my mind and body are my own, and what I do while you're away is my own business.

Larry, you are so good. Please write and tell me whether your head is decapitated or not. I shall be able to sleep infinitely better.

Are the Huns as good-looking as our natives? I mean the men, are they handsome? Not that I care; but I could not bear thinking of you killing handsome men. It would be ridiculous if my Larry were killing them. It would be as if he were killing himself. It would make the dream too horrible. Instead of one Larry lying in the grass bleeding, with dirty black flies tucking their children into the bed of his flesh, there would be fields and fields of you, smouldering with the heat of a thousand beautiful men.

For my sake, do not kill beautiful soldiers.

If your officer commands you to pierce their hairy bellies with your bayonet, and to use the butt of your gun on their tender lips, tell him that I play *Larry*, that I will not stand for it. That I will play *Larry* with as many of our natives as are dead enemy in the fields.

Larry, dear, when you kill the Hun, you go through his pockets, don't you? And you look in his wallet. Sometimes you find a photograph of a girl. I know you do. You must send them to me. I am here, isolated. I have a right to know how beautiful the sweethearts of the Hun are. I have a right to know if they are more beautiful than I. At least it would pick my spirits up to laugh at these photographs. Because I could look at them and know that their Larrys will not be coming back to them.

Oh, Larry, Larry, you must write soon. I have an awful feeling that you have become a paraplegic, or that your legs are cut off at the thigh... I see you bleeding in the grass, staring glass-eyed at the sky. Vultures with the faces of Mr. and Mrs. Meat hover in the air. Hyenas with Aunt Peelya's face grind their teeth at you. And fields and fields of beautiful Huns, all Larrys.

Write soon, if your hands have not been smashed by shrapnel.

Your sweetheart, with all my love, Miss Wimp

As I grow weary... You measure weariness, I shall take another way...

They cried, hullo, hullo, as I was going into my head. The shades were drawn on the downy sills. Only the blur of an underwater smile. The softness and the liquid of tears.

Beyond the mask the fat belly of a stooping woman, the squinting navel, the man sets forth through the grey hills that convolute like the brain.

Brooks purr. Ecstasy of wind touching a leaf. House which may not be a house. A group of birches. A cloud becomes a horse. Yes, the birch trees are a horse. Yes, the birch trees are a house which may not be a house.

It is thick, it is breathless, the flesh of the cloud; the hams and bellies of women. The cloud is joyous. It hums like a thousand voluptuous wasps.

A bell is calling. Through the draperies it calls. With butterflies emptying out of it. It throbs, tingling far from here within.

Road of the glorious corpse. Chicken bones and charred love letters fettered in a hangman's knot. They rattle in the breeze like whispering girls.

From telephone poles, hullo, hullo.

The dangling man flutters. The wind kisses his neck.

The dangling man turns slowly on a thread. The moon paints his face with ashes. Goodbye...

For a little while let me talk without your listening; a rehearsal inside of a dream...

I said, do not listen! If you dare, I shall confess a monstrous crime.

How dare you continue listening! Stop listening!

Shall I say a dirty word? Oh, no, dear sir, you shall not drive me to that. If you think for a minute because you are listening I shall commit myself to dirty words...because you expect an inclination, a childish temper...

No, calmly I say, Spring is coming. Make of that what you will. It implies, wouldn't you say (if I bothered to listen, which I assure you I can't, since I'm filled with my own shrieking) a certain passage out of the crystal madhouse?

The bird fled my land. The wind pouring through the naked trees. By the window in the hall, in the oyster-light of the winter shadow. Standing by the window, alone, alone, wearing corduroy pants, a woolen shirt, hair too long; by the window, saw the field in white the sky of grey, the field in white, the sky is darker. A black tree strikes the posture of grief... Dust-bound, my ankles are grey.

Now rising the iris blade, the green-killer's sword.
An army arises. Can't you hear the crumbling above the ascension?... The shuddering fipple of the bird?

The wind is full of girls. Softly they weave my flesh to sperm...

Now shall I describe my death... Not sure that this shall do it. May have to go beyond this... Perhaps I shall only give the reason to go on living...
But to say, to come dangerously near. God, what fun!
It was because there was nothing else, that my hands began to mate with one another. They tried the positions of fornication. What should I have done, formed them for prayer?

Love is a superstition that haunts the posture forever. The humpback is one frozen in fornication. The limping cripple is dancing eccentric rape.
Now I keep my bed linens, with her rose, forever. Cigarette butts, stained by her lips, are my dragon's teeth. My life is ritual. I am superstitious...

My words come, inverted kisses, drawn from me in this vacuum. I am being drawn inside out.

The World is a neuter monotony. As she loved me, I imitate myself.

Suddenly all is lost. I remember the softness of her inner thigh, her stomach against my face...

I weep, my fluid becoming cerebral...

They found a dead man, stabbed in the heart by his penis. His hands tied together by their fingers. A woman's voice bleeding softly from his ears...

Alfred

Now, as to the love affair...

She was the daughter of a military man; which doesn't hurt in the least.

The family name was Alfred. It was Alfred, no matter which one you talked of. It was Colonel Alfred, Mrs. Alfred and their offspring, Alfred.

Colonel Alfred's daughter was quite fat. I would have married her, but she was wrongly sexed. She was quite as fat as Colonel Alfred's daughter was, which in this case she happened to be. (I'm trying to get my bearings.) As is the daughter, so is the father, (more than at this time I cared to note), and so was the mother, the good Colonel's wife, who, on occasion, had said to the Colonel's offspring, do not tell anyone your name, I don't want them to know you are mine.

The Colonel was a very fat man in his own right; vain and given to rage. With thin legs and tiny feet in shiny footwear, boots of polished chestnut. With a horseshoe of yellow coils on the back of his head. He was vain and given to rage, as his little feet pranced with spiteful indulgence.

His wife would say, oh, do be still awhile, your little boots tick-tocking make me mad with longing for them to stop.

On rainy days when he could not go out Mrs. Alfred would search the memories of her youth, seeking things to entertain the Colonel. For the Colonel would be promenading with his pale, rain-soaked shadow, and stamping his booted little feet; until Mrs. Alfred would say, go to bed, Colonel.

Enough of this.

To continue... Then the spark. The moment of Alfred. We stole out one night, irresistibly drawn... As it was...under a heaving tree, in a sky of silver, he and I are heavy with the shadows of leaves, sweeping us like a stampede of mice.

So cool the night. And sailing there a coin of milk. In the west a city glows like embers on a grate.

My love is breathing in my arms as the wind breathes through a tree.

I put my ear to his lips to feel him breathe. He wets my ear and whispers he is near.

He is vile with love! *What is unclean shall be clean.*

We stood at the gate of death. Our heads lowered, humbled unto the other. Slaves without masters.

We stood before the gate of death. The gate opened on the garden of repulsion, where shit and the urine flower bloom. Ghastly in the silver of the moon. Upon a broken column the horned Cupid sits and farts!

His belly like another, softer moon, with its mother-scar...

I long for his bowels, his liver, his toes... He is my potency. I could seduce a God!

And then, not being able to live without each other, we set up housekeeping. And, of course, the way was down. What was fine for a night would not do for a week.

At first there was only a spiteful boredom between us. I remember a tablecloth. Upon it, porridge, pickles and the primrose. And there, Alfred, amid his yellow coils, chewing pickles and washing coffee through the residue; terribly overweight.

Sick, I remember, quite sick of the Chinese back-scratcher, the Viennese waltz, the corners of the room, and the way distance looks from the window.

Also, my wife (if you can call Alfred that) had a nose with two nostrils containing hair, through which the atmosphere was drawn upon.

He had an eye. Two of them. Several eyebrows, or so, which dominated his eyes. Being nearer heaven when he stood up.

These details seem too general, yet they are the few things I remember (not to mention his heft)...all that I am able to recall, save the yellow plumage on his head, with its loops and diversions and what all ...

He had fingers all over himself in the ministry of vanity, many of them. They had nails slightly dark with particles of previous moments; washed by night and filled by day.

The woman (I cannot decide about Alfred) whose ear I chose to snore into was not different; or *shall* not be different, as I project, twisting time, losing it, confusing the segment with the segment...

Of that morning: *And will you please pass the pickles before I get really angry!*

You're hurting my arm, whimpered Alfred.

Now began a series of skirmishes. I wanted to be free, and yet I feared to be alone.

Meanwhile, I discovered Alfred had a wife.

Alfred said, Alfred and Larry are my favorite people, all the others phooey! Alfred smiled with the wisdom of his mother and said again, Larry, you're the sweetest person I know...

(I was sure he was going to tell me about his wife.)

Does that mean you love me? I asked.

That would be telling, you cripple, replied Alfred.

I'm not a cripple, I said.

So what, said Alfred, does it matter if I think you're a cripple, or some woolly monster with bristly cheeks, with paws that sicken me for their cruel nails?

But it's plain I'm not a cripple, except in my right foot, which doesn't matter because 1 only use my left, hopping quite as nicely...

Never mind, screamed Alfred.

Are we in love? Is this an affair of love? Is our situation one of love? Is that our bond, our oneness? I asked.

If you don't leave me alone I shall grow to hate you, you jealous thing, screamed Alfred.

Who was that lady I saw you with last night? I asked.

That was no lady, that was my wife, you nosey thing, replied Alfred.

Tell me quickly that you love me better than yourself, I screamed.

Why should I lie?, asked Alfred.

And he left me.

Now came one of my first important illusions. I became Captain Love, and dispatched a letter to Alfred's wife. I wished to hurt her and to disgrace Alfred by describing a fool's death for him.

I have the letter here. I never sent it, though it's had plenty of use over the years as a sweat-cloth.

I shall read it to you: My dear Madam Alfred,

Necessity, endowed by duty...the necessity to end hope...

This is Captain Love speaking. (As if your eyes did not jump to the foot of the page immediately.) The name should be enough.

Apparently you understand before I speak, i.e., if my sympathy is all that I think it is.

How it was, as I must tell you, (my telling being your only memento) was as follows... But I warn you to indulge my station; to understand that as a man rises from the ranks so his tastes also rise. And before long, only the tongue of the nightingale will do for breakfast.

How is this had out to sea? You are foolish, madam (assuming you asked that question, I can do no more than repeat, you are foolish). Possibly the cargo, or the dollars-and-cents of it, suffered for the storage of live nightingales clucking in the holds. Until in a rage for the incessant clucking, I had them put overboard, to their amazement; realizing not at all, they, the nightingales, that so much of the earth's surface is water. But this is another matter...

As to that person whom you regarded as a husband (being uninterested as to the legality of that title) I knew him. Not as you, certainly not that! Under the right circumstances...had he been a duke...but why talk of dukes? there are many others who are dukes. The world is not poorer dukes for the loss of seaman Alfred.

I knew him, then, as an underling, a person one orders from the room. A person to whom one might have said, this is my boat, get off of my boat.

Myself, little acquainted with the workings of ships, my best navigational effort, I must confess (actually, I need confess nothing to you) is, on a clear night, to locate the Big Dipper. I can not tell what star in its formation points where, but I enjoy looking at it.

On finding it I am likely to raise an underling to my level for a moment by shouting, distracted with joy, look, there it is!

I return quickly enough to my official monotone, and dismiss them from the deck. I make them all go below, so that I can observe Heaven without their thick, warm, animality consuming and excreting about my ears. Never mind the reef!

I can not stand human beings. If I resemble one, (which I do) I make no effort to identify myself further.

Your husband treated me, I mean the heavens, like his personal chart room.

Your husband ate lumpy oatmeal for breakfast. He did not complain. The proof is his death.

On Wednesday afternoon, I had been crocheting a doily for Admiral Polyp's night table. My lavender scented cigarette was making me quite ill. And a small woman kept bothering me for a donation. (I show no charity and expect none to show me any.) We have no women on board, and so I assume I fainted for a moment from burning lavender. At any rate, as the nausea receded, a small hunger for lobster arose. Becoming stronger. Perhaps not as strong as you might think, as I am accustomed to believing my slightest whim equal to any other's most passionate desire. Which, if it is not, it becomes, because I am a very spiteful man. And if it means some strenuous effort for an underling, my whim becomes a giant, a passion.

Seaman Alfred, slave, dog, I must have a lobster, I said to your husband, go overboard, this is my boat (see, here are the papers) and do not return unless you are accompanied by a lobster.

We lost him at sea. First of all, I refused to wait for him because I was in a terrible rush to meet Admiral Polyp in the South Seas. Secondly, because my desire for lobster had subsided. Thirdly, I knew your husband would never find one anyway. And fourthly, I knew that my desire for lobster in the beginning was only a disguise for my real desire, to see your husband (if not to see, at least to know) drowned.

His death puts off mine. Somehow, if I feed Death, I am safe.

You think me silly, madam? Or is your grief so great that you cannot see me? Sincerely, Captain Love.

I remember running out of doors. And I kept running... It seems like yesterday... It might have been yesterday, had the years not proven soft, like rotten doors, keeping neither wind nor day.

Then went me, pouring in a thousand rhymed rivers.

Sometimes at night I lay, stagnant, dotted with stars. The frog of thought, peeling river scum, swimming through the meditation.

But, in a little, the earth gave way. And falling, I boiled, I seethed. I cried on the rocks. I ran through the wood, tangling my liquid hair in the faggots of the wood.

In a little, I slept again. I entered the earth, drowning in the marsh.

Was I ever the same river that started on the mountain?

Ah, then, the voyage... I might title it: Travel Notes Of My Recent Journey Out Of Mind.

...I mounted the great white stallion of the particular delusion, which at the time was an aeroplane flying in God's throne room.

Unsure, I mounted a snail, and began the slow descent through meditation, slowly, through the tentative rings made of smoke; the day I stood at the window, ready to scream. The rain falling down. And I was smoking many cigarettes.

Will he come? That is another question. Many, many questions...

I stood at the window, ready to form a scream, the crimson noise...

Soon the great ship was ready. I could see it across the room, stationed in the horizon of the wall. Dark. A dark ship it was, as all ships are.

I had to smile. I had to smile at my own smile. I believe what is not believable. Therefore, there is no threat of contradiction.

I admit I believe what is untrue. But your opinion is worthless.

Captain Bow Wow and First Mate Meow stood on a bridge in a Japanese garden, vibrating their fans like hummingbird wings.

The horse began to gallop. And below us the glittering lights of Star City.

…The snail is slow, but here I go…

I am discovered one lovely day at the window, screaming.

Father and Son

To introduce my father and his beautiful comportment. To show you briefly how he began to impress persons of position.

He began to make coronations, inaugurations, and all manner of high occasions his hangout; not to mention exclusive clubs and the homes of outraged occupants.

It was not unusual to hear such as this, get off my back, Gulping!

Father very often had a habit of perching on his friends' shoulders when he was trying to make a good impression. It could be quite unnerving, as father was not a small man.

Father came of an old family, which he traced back to Neanderthal, and was generally respected; but he had this one insistence, and before one knew it, he would be on one's shoulders.

Now father was holding his highball in one hand and a cigar in the other, sulking on Duke Shelby's shoulders.

You're getting ashes on my haircut! screamed Duke Shelby, to the astonishment of the gentlemen reading their newspapers.

A fat Colonel, recently from the colonies, sat in his bulging khakis; his face waxy and red. He put his paper aside and said, come down, Gulping, no one's going to hurt you.

But by this time father had fallen asleep.

He looks very peaceful, doesn't he, Shelby? remarked the Colonel.

Yes, he is a dear when he sleeps. You forget all his waywardness; he looks just like an angel, cooed the Duke.

But then Duke Shelby whimpered, I can't stand it, I feel weighed down. And he began to shudder, screaming, get off, get off, or I'll have you executed for treason!

Aw, let him sleep, soothed the Colonel, he's not hurting anybody.

But the truth was, father had put his lighted cigar on the Duke's haircut. Also, father's highball was beginning to spill from his sleep-disoriented hand.

I think I shall have to shake him, said the Duke.

Then father awoke and yawned, oh, hello everyone.

Get off my back, Gulping, cried the Duke.

Okay, I have to go to the bathroom, anyway.

Look out for my key chain! And if you stain my knickerbockers in the slightest, I shall declare my political position, roared the Duke as father climbed down.

And you will kindly take that offensive Havana product with you, too, the Duke snickered.

I would prefer to leave it here for when I next visit, said father.

Very well, said the Duke, but I can't be responsible if my eldest son sees it.

Nevertheless, countered father, I shall hold you responsible, and shall take due legal procedure if in any way it is tampered with.

Oh, take the foul thing with you, it's already burned a hole in my new haircut.

The fat Colonel in the bulging khakis came to attention and said, Shelby, I do really think a man has a right to leave his cigar in his bedroom, without its being smoked or maligned.

Well, answered the Duke, Gulping might have the decency

to use my ears, instead of letting his ashes drop on my sequined jacket and my hair shirt which my mother knitted for me. I have two ears, and it would be little inconvenience for Gulping to use them.

Father said, I'm going home, where I can get some real sleep.

Well, go along then, said the fat Colonel, who was beginning to feel uneasy because father had already mounted his shoulders.

I do really think going home is a capital idea, said the Colonel. I do really think it would be a splendid thing, and I'm not joking, he said again.

But father could not hear him, because father had fallen asleep.

You see, said the Duke, that's what I don't like about him. It's hard to keep his attention.

Get off my back, Gulping, cried the Colonel.

Oh, forget him, and have a drink, said the Duke.

Oh, very well. But I do wish he'd get off my shoulders—I'll have a double whiskey.

But as the Colonel was lifting his glass to his mouth, another hand guided the glass to another mouth.

Oh, damn, said the Colonel, he's having my drink in his bedroom.

But on winter nights, said the Duke, when you've foolishly forgotten your scarf, he's a blessing. The poor love him.

Nevertheless, said the Colonel, it's a hot night and the bastard's sweating profusely and so am I.

He also has a Boy Scout Insignia, said the Duke.

Oh, screamed the Colonel, that puts another light on it.

I should say it does, said the Duke.

And so on. And in such manner father began his career.

Speaking of using the shoulders of others (either for recreation or specific utility) it is brought to mind a certain rather lyrical military adventure of mine. Not to say father's was any the less, but rather to draw a parallel that points up our similarities, precious as is the blood kinship between father and son. The use of the shoulders of others seems to be a family trait...

At any rate, they were carrying my corpse, whose name was Buddy Butch, through the Forest Of The Old Man. Unknown to them, I think their names were Pink and Pratt, I was quite alive; sleeping and waking by turns, lighting cigarettes, putting them out on the shoulders of my bearers.

My code name was Buddy Butch. I was on a secret mission into enemy territory.

It seemed expedient to play dead at the boundary, most of my body on enemy territory, so as to make my enemies think I came from their side.

I was lifted up by two soldiers. At the time my eyes were closed. I could not tell whether I was traveling back into my own land, or being borne into enemy territory.

I was watching the stars, with my ears wide for gossip, for it had occurred to our soldiery that gossip is more important than military facts, which are likely to bore one to death, especially if one knows very little about the subject, which is the case with our military.

Rather, juicy bits of hearsay nourish tedious hours spent at Central Intelligence. Or swatting flies grown so thick lately around Colonel Muff's desk. I must tell Colonel Muff not to eat carrion. Or, during office hours, he shouldn't. It's an unpleasant thing at any hour. I shouldn't have tasted it were it not for the fact that he out-ranks me. Or does he? Self, are you a General? A King? That's even better.

Sergeant Pluck has a nasty way about him. Captain Girlish;

well, all right, but I don't like his long eyelashes. Should tell him not to wear carnations on his chest. It looks girlish for a military man to look like a flower queen. I mean, it's all right to wear roses in your hair in the evening, or high-heeled slippers in dress parade, or perhaps a little rouge. But, my goodness, a flower print gown, even if the weather is so warm; *and I really do need a fan*—such airs!

How I came up. Not by looking pretty for the generals. Crossing and uncrossing my legs a dozen times to attract attention to my legs. The hell with it, my ability is what counts. Not that I discount romance, or looking nice. Working in the latrines, I always had the scent of, well, just a trace, mind you, of an expensive perfume.

It was well known I spent most of my pay on fine perfume. I felt it was worth it as far as my morale and dignity were concerned. They called me *Skunk*.

Then I rose from the ranks. General Moon approached me one day and promoted me to King. No, wait, Private First Class. I entered the Intelligence.

General Moon suspected his wife of some moral inconsistency, which I was commissioned to check out, which later involved myself in such a way as to put the blame squarely on General Moon. Which proved to be another stepping-stone in my career.

By hook or crook I should've made it, since my star is lucky. Otherwise it wouldn't be, which is contrary to the course of my career, which clearly shows that if we have stars at all, mine is lucky. In other words, I either have a star or I don't. If I must be saddled with one, it is forced to be lucky, even if it isn't. If it isn't lucky it can't exist.

...Eating carrion. Why? Because the great birds of prey are known to be, in their off-moments, eaters of rotten meat; and

Colonel Muff thinks of himself as being a great eagle?

No, he is a lame chicken who saves a dime on hamburger by eating decayed entrails, and pieces of newspaper. He picks a juicy murder to chew on. He says there's a little blood if you chew hard enough. But it is always yesterday's newspaper; he seems to have little chance of getting away from carrion.

These two under me are talking about Corporal Smooch's underwear. It sounds choice.

They know I'm not dead, which makes things easier. I had begun to get lonely. Soon they will put me down and make me walk. Or will they pretend to think I'm dead to keep me off guard? What's the difference? The night is beautiful, and I enjoy riding on their shoulders. I look up, wondering which star is mine, while branches full of birds float by. (Or, are they bats?) Silver leaves, made silver by the moon. Fences trailing off behind us down the road. An occasional cow in a silver field. A house, and a string of smoke rising out of it.

...Captain Girlish and his jade brooch... All right, all right, roses in your hair in the evening. High heels are not unbecoming the uniform; strapless heels can add a certain flare. A touch of rouge, but not carnations in Central Intelligence. They never learn.

If these two rogues carrying me think I don't know they know I'm playing dead, they're sadly mistaken. I not only know it, but I enjoy their knowing it, because I hate secrets. When you have a secret, you know you must tell it. Secrets are designed to draw attention to themselves, which, of course, leads to their revelation. Things are designed to become precisely what they are not. Otherwise they shouldn't exist at all.

Now these rogues seem to expect I shall be happy in a hole

that they are standing by. It would be cozy, I must admit, but I'm not ready to go underground just yet...or, are they calling my bluff...?

They know I know they know I live. Well then, let's see how far they intend to carry this mischief. Their commanding officer shall receive an angry note by messenger. And I assure you, by tea time I shall be invited to imbibe rare wines as an apology, which I shall refuse for the sake of beer, which is quite a favorite with me.

Of girls, suddenly they spring to mind like birds of the summer before. No doubt I shall be married before my life is out...

Now, I really must concentrate. This gossiping with oneself is all very well with a glass of tea on a summer's eve, when the birds are becoming quiet.

An occasional shriek, as if someone had his claws stepped on in a nest. Or an anxious flutter, as if having one's claws stomped on weren't enough, but now, accompanying it, the discomfort of having to unfold one's wings to ward off a dangerous fall. Yet, one feels that finally there is room for all...

I sip my tea again and smile, Why not? If it weren't for these mosquitos...but the fumes of the rose...Eternity sums itself in this sweet moment ...

What we are after in our official capacity is gossip. Some blow to man's international sense of morality. Something that will stir the old woman in every general.

Every young supple girl whom you might well marry, must become in time the old woman with vertical wrinkles surrounding her mouth...

For a moment I shall do a sub-portrait. It could almost take on the form of a last will and testament. It goes, when I was little, and lay in the evening under a sheet, I watched a great ghostly tent arise from the pit of my legs.

I was dying. I was seeping into a point that rose toward Heaven. I could hear the birds, and then I slept...

When I appeared as Madam Pastridge, they jeered. When I appeared as the Duke of Ambrey, they said, sweep the back porch. So I moved on.

I set up shop in Eversville. Falling in love, I spoiled my comfort, and set fire to several buildings on my way out of town...

I grow sick. My parts begin to set up shop for themselves. Many, many twilights... Darkness...

I shall leave my evening dresses to the evening; they shall find an escort in the wind. They shall be wafted through the fields in the evenings like fine ladies, ladies that I could never be...

I leave my Dukedom and my trinkets (my typemetal Eiffel Tower, my necktie with the nude girl on it, my piece of wedding cake, etc.) to be discovered centuries from my time, far from the jealousies that have covered over what I hold most dear.

That I sicken, that every organ malfunctions as each organ contradicts the other, pulling me asunder.

I hear my bones breaking in the night.

My heart, having come loose, falls like an autumn leaf into my stomach, tangles in my lymph, down into my thigh, strangling in my calf... Not long now...

Madam Palepun, who loves everyone. Madam Passpie, who they accused of being a man. Madam Bairbonnie. The Duke of the Evening Mist, who wandered down by the canal, who never wished to be born, had never asked to be born…just where the sewer empties on the river. The children play there in the evening.

They say the unmarried woman across the way is to have a child. A sixteen-year-old snip hit his father and ran away with the rent money. I said, you goddamn sonofabitch, stop pawing me…

At the window, I told them off. I know exactly what you are; I know that each of you laid a pound of shit last Monday, except you constipated bastards. I know that Mr. Marlboro sits to pee. It's fairly obvious, he leaves the seat down on the hallway toilet.

I spit down on them.

The children throw stones up, wreaking my flesh, breaking my fingers.

As I was saying, fuck you and you and you, they threw a stone into my mouth, which I swallowed.

The landlady, who thinks I'm a movie actor…

In my last moment a faraway city glitters. And I hear the quarreling of angels close by. I am drifting, as it were, sifting… outward…

Here it is, the cherry seeds in me bloom. Apples aspire to trees in my bosom. The invasion of the new order. Overrun with strange powers!

I shall go down and buy a hamburger, and then, I swear to

you, I shall die. After, of course, my cigarette...and then I think I can sleep.

I shall pull my tentpole. I shall pull, pull, pull...

Goodbye. I was the Duke of Maypole.

Another military episode, which will display something of mother. And which will instruct you of my unfailing devotion to duty, in spite of the fact that it is a rare man who knows his duty, myself included.

I will use the name Rosemari in order to disguise myself a little. It was Cavalry Captain Rosemari on a purple pony, lost from the battle, waiting in a birch white forest.

The Captain, that was I, was checking his uniform for maggots. His pony gave an impatient snort.

Now don't you start on me, said the Captain.

Poor stuff, my equipment, said the Captain, good enough for a Swiss child...no doubt quite charming in those circumstances; a little girl wearing a sky-blue shawl and pink boots... she is riding a purple pony; and like my pony, her pony has a red saddle with bells and streamers; and because it takes nothing away from the utility of the pony, he wears a little straw hat like my purple pony... Indeed, this is no mount for a military man!

Having been given the name of Rosemari by a blind mother who never understood my sex.

Lacking sight, she turned to touch, reading braille late into the night by candle light.

As to my sex, she could never give herself to that exploration.

Like a long term sunset (which describes my hopes) I blush continually. Less than a blush, less than my constant embarrassment, people should say you're not looking your old self. The facade of my health is shame. Shame because they think the pony with the red saddle is good enough for *him*...bells and streamers!

Once at the battle of Fluckers, I was given a rocking horse! I never left the barracks, but I was ordered to stay in saddle until the battle was over.

My fellows came back from the field singing, their chestnut mounts glowing like copper, their sabers aloft, like cataracts above their heads. I, found foolishly rocking to and fro near my cot on a rocking horse.

Certainly, I had done my duty. I had rocked my guts out, I was quite seasick; my pigtails dripping with sweat.

My mother kept saying, Rosemari, dear, you'll have bad dreams, you're getting too excited.

It was explained by the authorities that I had been stationed to guard the barracks. And, as far as the rocking horse, well, mere form, no more. Being a soldier of the cavalry, a captain, no less (Captain Rosemari) all in all it seemed proper and fitting that I should be mounted.

A real horse, although more dignified, might in these circumstances have been less useful, owing to its odor and manure properties, etc.

It was explained away by the higher authorities, but it did not lessen my feeling of inadequacy. Especially when they were passing out sabers and it came my turn to receive one, and they were all gone. No one can be blamed. Unseen forces, perhaps? I took the wooden sword with good grace, and revered it as if it were metal; and I used it just as bravely. And I will go on using it in defense of Honor and Country.

Not so much the weapon, as the man... All such little sayings lighten the load.

Now my pony looks around, with its large brown eyes. Perhaps he is trying to read the newsprint on my hat ...

Flower

Let me tell you about a memorial dinner held in honor of the late Professor Flower.

Someone rose, glass in hand, and said, there was once a very wonderful person, named...for God's sake be careful, or you'll spill my head, the way you're tipping it, like to lose my wits. Here, pour it in this cup...anyway, his name was...if you don't stop, Shirley, I shall call the doctor that delivered Miss Mirk's hat out of Shrill's well-shaped thing, which is altogether much better than yours...

No, no, I mean... It goes like this, we sat down to celebrate the passing of that wonderful person. A memorial dinner in honor of a very wonderful person. Gasser, beginning to pass air through the rattan of his chair, raised his voice to *C* above middle *C*.

Someone hit his mouth with a hammer. We clapped our hands at the beauty.

Stand up, everyone, and salute...

No. Perhaps someone merely read the Professor's most important work aloud to the members of a society known as The Flower Club: *An Autobiographical Report*, by Professor Flower: I am living in the year one thousand, nine hundred and something, A.D.... Help!

Your beloved old Professor, Polly Flower

Someone rose to make another toast, here in zephyr den, here at no place, here at X, zero, Nth degree, limit, infinity; here and here... There!

To this someone said, oh, dear, draw door, window, eyelid, mind, because the winds are knocking with chubby hands. Oh, dear, such an empty place, there are no doors. Everything is made of wind. The doors are made of wind. The wind is made of wind.

And was answered, please don't be realistic, or fatalistic, or catastrophic. Please, please, please...

And then someone said, come, kiddies, time to laugh and roar. Time to get real caught in the laughing-sillies.

And was answered, what is he saying? You stop saying anything. The wind is most dreadful in the afternoon, because there is no afternoon. Where is morning? What is noon, or soon?

Molecules make you sick. The dizzy night, I can see, but up over heaven through star sheath I think I begin to speed, boiling and spilling.

The thin ones so shrunk by birth several times. Each time more soul. One time it'll be a puff of smoke out of the slime sweet belly of old Grandma Flower. And all that fuss for nine months, and then only a little puff of smoke...

Someone debated, may I say *a tree?* Yes, I may say *a tree.* No, I may not say *a tree.* I shall do exactly as I wish, *tree, tree, tree* ...

Someone asked, do you have a cigarette for my head? My head wishes to blow smoke through its nostrils.

Someone answered, blow air through your pants.

And then someone asked, are you trying to put me into a trance? You are succeeding. Whispering in grey, angel-ladies, dancing in nightgowns of snow...

I think I'd better talk about Minor Bliph and Roger Snore, who decided to do nothing. Minor moved his chair up to the window. Roger aimed a gun at the back of Minor's neck.
I have eyes in the back of my head, said Minor.
And what do you see? asked Roger Snore.
None of your business, Roger Snore, said Mr. Bliph.
I think enough has been said about Roger Snore and Minor Bliph.
After all, it's Professor Flower...

...Or, the man under a crown, which goes: A man under a crown ordered, all of my orders are to be obeyed under threat of disorderly conduct.
Oh, yes, we hear you, most important creature in the universe.

...Or, a bit of hearsay: during the famine Milly began to eat Grandfather Flower. They warned her that the stories about the Great Indian War and the Chicago Fire would be curtailed by the destruction of Grandfather.
What do I give a damn for all the old geezer's talk? Milly said, as she gnawed on his head as he was trying to read the latest reports about the famine in his paper.
Leave Grandfather Flower be, they would say, he has many coughs to cough.
But one day Milly bit Grandfather's Adam's apple off his stringy neck.
But this is no end of it. Wait...

Let me tell you about a memorial dinner held in honor of the late Professor Flower...someone rose, glass in hand...

Let me tell you about a memorial dinner held in honor of the late...someone rose, glass in hand...someone rose, glass in hand ... Enough!

I hate you, Doctor Flower, almost as much as my father hated me; no less than I hated my father, or he hated you.

But to my career, which leads us nicely to death. That meditation... And of mother... My penis... To death.

We were set out against the enemy, dressed in the colors of the wood. The vegetable pretense.

We console ourselves with shrubs, for we can not tell them from men.

Oh yes, we are crying. Not having asked to be born, we have no wish to undo our births. In fact, we are asking to be born. Though born without consent, we are now giving our consent.

It is when we break from our neutrality we risk the contradiction.

Are birth and death an arc separate from the circle?

We are asking to be born. Disguised as vegetation, we are trying to be men.

Yes, we are crying. Blowing my nose into an oak leaf, reminding myself of mother with her handkerchief at my farewell. I could not tell whether or no she was smothering laughter. It seemed she was upset by an indigestion conveniently wrought to hide from herself the grief that she felt, yet having the appearance to strangers of undisguised grief; which has the effect of satisfying everyone, both my mother and strangers. Except that I could not help noticing vomit running out of her handkerchief.

No, actually, I think, thinking back, it was an old tramp

smelling strongly of liquor was vomiting. No, it was not mother. Mother was roaring with laughter to see her little soldier going forth.

My life is independent of mother. It has its own wish to be. It is, in a way, in competition with mother, as with other life.

It was not mother, I think, but a tramp who vomited surreptitiously into his sleeve.

Now the shrubs no longer console in our advance, for the enemy, too, has on the colors of the wood. Every shrub and blade of grass bears the sign of the assassin.

Even I, in the wood, moving, am dangerous to myself.

If I lie quietly as insects crawl on my lips, and think only of mother, I may survive like the trees and the constancy of the brook.

An open charge has an unasked to be born feeling about it.

But here, sneaking up on the enemy, and destiny closely observed ... I am afraid to be born and yet somehow afraid not to be.

And somehow the question of man, aside from his death or his crisis...the question of man, which, of course, is his death, which is his crisis. Somehow more than the present battle or the camouflaged flesh...

Perhaps it is the heat, and the uncertainty of the grass and the danger of trees...

I think of mother, as if casting my anchor.

...I am not afraid of death, only I don't want some sonofabitch to kill me.

I hate to be startled. It makes my heart beat fast, and gives me the discomfort of fearing death intensely for a moment. It destroys my calm appraisal of man's fate as regards his death. My biology suddenly asserts itself; and it scares me to think I will scream and kick when death really comes.

Fear proves to me that I am really afraid. I am afraid to be afraid, which does not stop me from fearing. And it grows; fear breeds the fear of itself.

...And still, the fear of being *that* afraid. Until one will tremble like a fool.

Any blade of grass may swell into a bayonet. No less than the miraculous becoming of my penis.

It is comfortable to think now of my penis.

And it may rain.

Rain!

It is to rain in summertime.

Tell us how it is to die in the summertime.

For it will rain...

Listen. It is listening for the rain.

When will it rain?

It will rain on Sunday, when I wandered through the place I had never been before, and heard the thorn-vine rasp its spurs on the grey house.

The light of the day is milky, then it will rain on the hayfork.

The brook is full of vulvas of silver, softly it moves with clefts and folds through the leaf dark of the wood. The deep breath of sleep through cedar and pine.

What is it to die in the summer?

For it will rain soon, and it is very far from home in a quiet avenue of some turning in a place we had never been before.

When it will rain, he whispers in a grey house. When in the electric rain of August, and hell zigzags across the meadow, he whispers deep under time. For that is long ago, and the door swings loosely in the high grass around the stoop.

And what is it in summertime to die?

It is to hear laughter in a garden, and the cannon-blast of distant thunder, and to wonder when it will rain; and bright butterflies fluttering in the cloud-dark of the garden; and that heavy sigh that precedes the desperate weeping. It is waiting now for the rain.

For that is a long time ago, and deeply under time, as we are waiting. And the door swings loosely in the high grass. Where I was was in a place I had never been before.

And when you die is that when it will rain?

It will rain on the hayfork. The hands are bones. The rain erases GULPING.

The wind is moving in a tree, and now it must surely rain, for to die in the summer is to have heard laughter fluttering in the sunshine through the scarlet avenues of the rose garden.

The sick man is covered with chalk-dust, and now it rains. All in silver blindness; no one may see, for it is surely raining in the meadow where the hayfork becomes dust.

What would you like me to talk about today, Doctor Flower?

Anything you wish.

Then, Doctor Flower, let us talk about you.

I never gossip about myself with anyone except my puppydog.

I wish only, Doctor, to chloroform you with my amazing insight, and mount you, like a butterfly, in your own museum of definitions.

Why do you wish to hurt me, you vicious and cruel madman?

Because I receive a severe pleasure, bordering the ecstasy my woman refuses me, to injure Mr. God and His creation, which has injured me more than I can it.

But I am not God.

Aren't you, Mr. Doctor of mental wizardry, author of all creation, prime mover of the bird at wing, the pitter-patter of the fox walking its trail...?

I am only a poor man, as yourself...

Play it humble, Doctor, like they taught you at Heidelburg, and then maybe I'll tell you a secret.

A blush-worthy secret, no doubt, you cruel and crazy madman.

You cannot make me weep, Doctor, with all your eloquence. You are in a sentimental rut, which you think will tickle the fine fibers of my innermost heart to wild bursts of humorless confession, which you would take down in your notebook, which you would read to your young daughter, so to enhance your standing in her childish eyes. To prove to her that you have vital information concerning certain persons, and that you yourself are a person of great excellence for this. And, as your daughter applauded you, you would weep and say you are the best person in the world...

Enough! You are moving me to the moment of anger when I shall do some unethical thing to your person. Which shall prove me to be a madman. Which at all cost I must control. Because, like you, I have a strong tendency toward madness.

As you say, Doctor. And like you (as the shoe fits the other foot) I am very much the doctor. Enough, at least, to realize that an insane asylum approximates your mental condition enough to warrant further consideration as to the means to be employed towards your further mental derangement.

You are looking for trouble, which I promise you will take the form of extreme violence to your person, which will render you incapable of further demonstrations of your amusing power to see the truth as I see it.

Doctor, I must admit, mortal combat with you would have its risks; but if the question arose as to which of us must die, I would prefer your death over mine, for the simple reason that

I fear to die more than anything else in this world.

Your death takes on many forms...now we're onto something, let us continue...in the clinical report on you, there seems to be many indications of an ambition far surpassing your native abilities. How would you account for this?

I felt driven by certain inadequacies in my upbringing to give my parents the things I never had.

Wasn't it, rather, that death takes many forms, and that we flee it by a thousand ambitions, and that we are at cross-purposes to ourselves through the hidden fission of our ambivalence? Whilst, on the other hand...and so, to continue...but perhaps...

Shut up, Doctor! For a moment I thought you were on to something, but I see you're still in your sentimental rut.

Stop that! I mean it! Now, if I'm going to help you, you must help me...

Well, all right, Doctor, but no more digressions into your own sordid affairs.

...To continue. And that the negation of the image we have of ourselves causes fear and confusion. An inability, finally, to decide on any action, because any act may lead to still further negation. So that, finally, we give up the world for the comparative safety of our own minds. We become immobile, and sit for long periods until somebody moves us.

That sounds good, Doctor. It's quite impressive, and might do well at a ladies' luncheon or an office party; or perhaps your young daughter might look with awe at your mouth. But I have been watching your hands, and their reminiscent motions, usually associated with a solitary act that young boys perform in the initiation of a certain function, which later will take on a more community aspect in the form of marriage and the propagation of the species. If you follow what I mean, Doctor?

I know what you mean!

Don't blow your top, Doctor! I didn't mean to imply that I know more about sex than you. I only meant that perhaps you're a fiend. That perhaps your sexual instinct had been arrested at some perversion. And that you had, and again, perhaps, separated love from sex, and that now only sex remained in some dark street of lonely sensation.

How dare you say I don't love my wife!

I didn't say it. You said it, Doctor.

And I'll say it again! I'll say it all I like!

Doctor, you will soon be screaming, and I hate that pretentious display of vocal power. And so, I must leave you, hoping I shall not return...

Father

Here is father. I have gotten no place in my life. Let's see how far he can get. Let's use his own papers and my speculation. And for the motor let us use your eyes and ears, fluttering in their murk, and we shall have a sort of motorcycle.

I have a bit of a treasure. Not only have I many papers of father's but, and manifold reasons for rejoicing (let the people of the land set up great tables in the streets, and let there be a day of feasting) I have a document of father's *father*. A thing, even for its few words, of greater encouragement than the very wink of God.

Here is father... Should he weep? He will giggle. No, he will be quiet for ten minutes, then he will say, la la la. He will look in a mirror. No, he will stand on a chair and jump to the floor. He will do exactly what he wishes, while looking over his shoulder.

He will lose his mind when he is alone in a room. He will bounce it on the wall and catch it in his mouth like a rubber ball.

He will wonder about dignity...

Suddenly, if he does anything, why should he do it? He questions, but why should he do it?

Suddenly he does it, because why should he question?

If he does anything, why should he do it?

He does nothing, which always means he will soon be doing

something.

But he is always doing nothing, which is restless indeed, it is too much like doing something.

He cannot help doing something. He will stretch the corners of his mouth with his fingers, like Mr. Flower does.

He is suddenly sick of Mr. Flower.

What can he do? Walk on coals, and burn his tootsies?

Now, should he weep? What shall he do after he weeps? Wipe his eyes and begin to laugh? And then what shall he do?

He will twitch like Mr. Flower does. Just like that.

I might as well insert grandfather's document at this point. It serves to regenerate father.

Dear Goose, This is your papa, dead forty years, just lately come to light (obviously so, assuming this to be your first reading).

You are well into the shabby middle years. You are a spinster, if I tell rightly. The child you were leaves little doubt as to your eventual failure.

You have by now most likely exhausted the frontiers of the family house. There are by now no ghosts, save yourself, fast dissolving out of life, as biology accounts us.

You come upon this by mail, as so arranged by me, from the law firm, if I remember rightly, of Dud and Wylly, along with certain family heirlooms, which I will not account here.

Love, that is how you fail.

You search the hallways...your mother and I linger, young, there...arm around her waist, we are looking down the main hall...the front door is open...and the call of the calling bird... the sway of trees...summer and the rose in scent...your mother...

You are a humpback. And became a very bitter young woman. Studious, yes, much moved by literature.

A particular professor (a Mr. Flower) moved your heart, praised your work, made you his favorite. You loved him, dreamt he came to you at night.

The passing of university days into educated and lonely boredom... Now, coming to a close, a dreadful life.

I, who am bones, past caring, mindless, laugh at you. Your papa.

And then father felt inclined to write to that darling Mr. Flower, the great spiritual father, that horrid monkey on his back. Not that he ever sent this letter. Unless this is a copy he kept.

Let us speculate on whether or not he sent it. Would it have changed anything?

Dear Mr. Flower, My beautiful woman has left me. Her nakedness has put on its clothes and is crossing the world.

If my bed were not smaller than the world, I would leave it, because it is too big now that her nakedness is gone.

Dear Mr. Flower, you seem to live in books.

Oh, great scholar, the children see you pick your nose, even though you keep it in a book, because, oh great scholar, you cannot help looking over your shoulder, because, oh great scholar, you are very right to remember beautiful women.

Do you think poets write poems? Or do poems create their poets?

Oh, Mr. Flower, why is it you know nothing?

Do you substitute your pillow for a woman?

You press your flower in a book.

Wise, gentle fool, bachelors grow old, and common folk ask, what use are poems?

What use *are* poems, Mr. Flower? Your student, George Gulping.

P.S. If you can make it, please visit me this coming Thursday. G.

Now I must go directly into the texts of father, these darling scraps of paper used as rags through the years, almost as if anointing myself, wiping away various forms of refuse; toilet tissues and the like...

A little diary covering the time between three Thursdays: Thursday. Waiting for Mr. Flower... I am so excited. I straighten my hair a dozen times. I pace. I see a trace of dust. I rub it away with my fingers.

He'll soon be here! He's coming, walking closer. He, in himself.

He. And soon I will see the doorknob turn and he will be here.

I glance in the mirror. My hair amiss. Any moment. It could be now. The doorknob could turn now!

Oh, where is he?

Friday. A dreadful calm. I have lived his arrival too much. If he comes now, I shall be a delayed bomb. A slow fuse. I shall explode with passion in time.

For a moment I am ready.

Monday. Not yet. A weekend of dreams. I hoped he would come as I slept. I now understand, only by a miracle will he come.

He does not mean to come. Only if he makes some mistake. Perchance to pass my door, remember me; drops in for a moment. I shall make some tea.

It is best not to expect, that is the way to make things happen.

It is a game, one must sneak up on oneself.

I'm tired. Will take a nap. Perhaps I shall awaken, My hand in his; well worth the waiting. Silly to think he wouldn't come ...so happy...

Wednesday. A knock at the door today. Could have been him, only he wouldn't knock.

A telegram signed, *The Animal.* Mildly shocked. *The Animal?* ...beast or man?

It said, are we not all the food of something else?

I have locked the windows and the door.

If he comes...if I'm asleep, the beautiful surprise. Him, here, sitting on my bed, my hand in his, all made right, waiting having been worth it.

The Animal makes it necessary to lock the doors. I should give up all hope. Life more bearable.

Thursday. Today I received a package. Brown paper and twine. A hat. His hat. His shoes. His watch, pants, underwear; gold fountain pen ... who could part him from this?

Friday. God, will the rain ever stop?

Definite sounds of an animal at the door. I heard it trying to force under the door and through the keyhole.

I would give anything not to be alone.

Saturday. I looked through the keyhole, the hallway seems overgrown with plant life. And I saw a grey animal. It seemed to be able to tell my eye was to the keyhole, because it suddenly leapt as I jumped away.

Mouth foam oozed through the hole. I'm sorry to have drawn attention to myself.

I have put the dresser and the vanity table against the door. I'm thinking strongly of suicide.

Monday. I have put on his clothes. It is almost as if he were holding me in his arms. I am surrounded in his smell, and the things that have touched his intimacy.
I have decided to jump out of the window tomorrow.

Tuesday. It is impossible to wait any longer.

Wednesday. I am still waiting.

Thursday. Last night I threw open the door and windows and waited in my bed.
Today I received a letter: Sorry to be late, dear. Have come into some money, so have sent my old clothes on. Forgot to take my pen out of suit jacket. Will be home tomorrow with a very unusual animal. Very unusual. It can talk and write. Signed, Flower.

I am leaving tonight. I am leaving the city. I can wait no longer. We build monsters when we wait...

Some pre-travel notes: I hadn't thought to go any place until I thought of it...and still I cannot think of it.
Where to go? How conduct myself to receive praise of posture or carriage under the sun of journey's end.
Shall I be bumpy on cobbled streets in shadow's fall? Or smooth as leopard's pelt on sands, looking like a sailing boat in my blowing burnoose?

Shall I pack my head in a separate box? And if I am a bird,

where are my feathers?

You, in the mirror, interest me no less than I interest you. Or did you think that? I haven't the slightest doubt that you are planning your own journey. Only, I don't think you are quite capable of existing without me.

I don't think anything shall happen unless I am there. Be that as it may, I am certainly going *there*...

Am I going anyplace? At least I am someplace. (or am I?) Perhaps I have arrived.

If I have been before this time, then I have arrived out of someplace.

Shall I pack my head in a separate box?

You, in the mirror, are no less interested, remember that.

It is to make something. Something out of stone. No doubt, a monster's head.

But why cut the stone? The head remains inside like a treasure. One can always cut the stone, this is called talent.

But what is that? The head is still there, whether talent or no.

Of heads...shall I pack mine in a separate box?

I think I shall pack all the equipment in a single box. The hands ... no, better leave them out to open the box. The feet, surely, the trunk, and the legs. I'll keep the feet on the legs... easier that way.

Lash the hands with wire with the address tag.

I'm beginning to think if going.

I am beginning now...

A document out of Africa: We sighted the man-eater. My rifle lay on a camp stool. The man-eater rushed towards us.

The porters fled. I quickly downed a glass of scotch, scientifically calculating the speed of the man-eater, time enough to down my scotch, pick up my rifle, shoot.

Except for the impotent click of the hammer, all went well. I'd forgotten to load the rifle.

The man-eater, for a moment in his charge, hesitated, stumbled, as if in the first stages of mortal wound. But seeing this time it was to be different, gained his speed again.

Confusion!

One eye being left in my crushed and torn skull...watching the man-eater eat me.

When the man-eater belches (for he has finished eating) I can see the blue sky, as I disintegrate.

I am now in a state of stools. I have lost all mobility, but can still reason.

...Again I am being eaten, this time by flies.

The porters peep through the bushes, and seeing the man-eater gone, come into the clearing.

They examine my gun, shake their heads with sadness. It seems the gun was loaded; I'd forgotten the safety-latch... By rights, this is my victory. The man-eater is dead. I pour another scotch, down it, instruct the porters (kicking the man-eater, to prove him dead to the porters) to skin the man-eater, to dress the head and paws.

At least there is a valuable lesson here: know your weapons completely.

Although, logically, this is my victory (forgetting the safety-latch is beyond consideration) it must be remembered that I *did*, and that I am the stools of the man-eater, and soon shall be the stools of flies; flyspecks, which you shall take to be vegetable lice on a tropical leaf in the Tropic of Capricorn...

And so...

But, again...

Oh, well...

A fly speck anywhere may be the Great Hunter.

What I wanted to say... I've forgotten what it was.

Father was also a butterfly hunter, and left a lovely treatise on the subject, which I think will go a long way in showing the mechanical talents of this universal man: You will observe, Doctor... I am not a Doctor, and no one was in the room saying this to me. But I was saying this to myself as I prepared to repair my heart, which I lost years ago to a woman who spurned me.
    And, having no heart...the woman?...there was no woman... Love was never unfortunate to me. For there has been no adventure of the heart. Perhaps that is why I have no heart. Or, it has atrophied in favor of my digestive organs, which lately, perhaps from over use, have needed considerable medication, commencing from both ends of the tract...

I was on a mission to extract a particular butterfly from some unspecified tropical wood.
    I set several bear traps, as I was not fit, nor have I been since my eating habits were fixed in early youth, to engage in hand-to-hand combat with butterflies.
    I had had the porters (or was it Chef Du Bois?) prepare a

meal of some proportion. Nevertheless, sipping my rye and beer between servings of spaghetti and pigs feet, I began to think of the woman God had meant me to love. Meaning, the only woman I would ever love; and how she might have saved me from the butterfly hunt.

True enough, I address myself as Doctor when speaking directly to myself. And, life being as it must be, (for who can say it should be any different? For if it were, it should still be as it must be, or something like it). As I say, I am not a Doctor, but who can say I might not have been one, had I been one, or something close to it. Might I not be considered, Doctor of Self? A study I have constantly applied myself to. Let the matter rest.

Fire does not fight fire. Fire might well encourage fire, except in cases where it doesn't. You might say that the fragility of the butterfly demands (unless that term is too strong, and would be happier said as, whispers) a fragile technique to be employed in hunting them. But it is their very delicacy that cries out against gentleness.

They are, for all their delicacy, what might be called *dangerous game*. Easily no contest for man's physical strength. But what is that? Neither am I. While being a fine butterfly killer... I dare say there hasn't been a butterfly invented that I cannot easily put to death. Deep breathing, naturally, is the answer. Physical fitness, which I admit I am lacking, but owning enough to make me more than a match in close quarters with them. Not that they are not as physically fit in their small way, perhaps more so, in their small way. But, *small*, that is it. They are definitely smaller, and, because of that, suffer in all contests of strength with man.

What they lack in strength they have in cunning.

Imagine chasing a butterfly, and then suddenly losing him. Where has he gone?

How they do it I shall never know. But suddenly the bright creature is inside, in your head, spreading the powders of its brilliance helter skelter. Pastel dreams move in on the manly hunter, the boudoir swims in its silks with the perfume of woman's flesh.

Therefore, I prefer to hunt them for my collection with bear traps and an elephant gun. I prefer not to think of the woman God meant me to love.

Now, Doctor, stop rambling and finish your food.
Yes, Doctor, I shall do that very thing.

From father's musical diary: Today I shall play magnificent treble with basso heart. Fart, the distant heads of thunder!

Rain in a falcon's span. The rabbit ran. Froze. Began to doze.

My it is boring under the sporing of flora. I rose early, like a schism between between and between.

Today I shall play raspberry splash, in all the blood colors of crescendo.

I must clean my lips to blow my lute. My hands for flute. My Adam's fruit most mute.

Orchestra, oh orchestra...

...Reiteration of promises to mother...

The subject: Birds on limb practising a child's piano scale.

All is quiet, and then I shall shriek to clear the world for music. A pathfinder ...

Oh God, shall I play beautifully. Rising and leaving my colleagues with only their scores?

Perhaps I shall lay aside the mechanism of my angel and reiterate promises to mother.

...A mosaic of sound, faint, powdery, like clouds under a

summer's moon...silence...the theater opening into the quiet reverie of summer woods at night...not but a firefly combusting like an ancient bell in a distant land...

Should I take, instead, whilst the monster of the orchestra roars in the cage of its theater, a turn into the wood? The quiet birch avenues under the dripping boughs of Spring, hearing feathered flutes, and the polite conversations from the brook as it talks to itself by the bank, through the rocks, the argument through the branches of a fallen tree, its quiet eloquence, its return to glass...

Knowing in mind, the beast roars. It writhes in all the agonies of departure. Returning on its strings; monstrous, the hideous whale; kettledrum heart, piccolo eyes, screaming; its brass lungs, violin claws of silk, its saliva run to oboes and flutes, mouth foamy with symbols...

I rose early. Checking the score... Paring my nails... Designing my hair in arrangements to disguise its loss...

I screamed, and that is how I came full turn around. Retiring, after all, with sweet prayers. ...And goodnight to mother, and all that I might have done that day I rose so early to play magnificent treble with basso heart...

The Death of Flower

Now father begins to rest.
I speculate.
Now father was alone. A man at the window.

When it rains, the window is a weepy cheek, with those terrible passive runs of grief. Blurry are the trees warped; and houses crumbling in wet. Yes, the world is oozing. Quite sweet, if the bird will sing. And the bird will sing, or shriek, like rusted hinges, opening.

Now all the birds crowd the sky with hag-scold.

If you pretend not to see him, you will see him in his thirtieth bachelor year. You pretend to be looking at the wet-wash kicking by an apple tree, and you see him; and he has been a long time alone.

You catch him by the window, by pretending to read the clouds (the angel hieroglyphic of zero) and you catch him, his arms on the sill. Now you think of his mother and his underwear. Now you think of the saliva in his mouth. You think of the fly in the hour, the hour of when, which came between the crisis and the crisis, the channel. It was quiet and the fly was buzzing. And the only thing remembered of the hour is the fly that was buzzing. Which reminds one of the clock, the white face and the black numbers, the black hands and its black frame; the white wall.

What they said is never what one imagines. One does not remember the words exactly. One does not remember the parts of what one remembers. One remembers very little, except that they were talking, and the fly that was buzzing.

The markets were busy. Was it coffee? Yes, and they stirred it with spoons. Cigarettes, no doubt. Then it was half-past ten. Then it was morning time. A fly is buzzing. A clock is ticking. Certainly it is raining. A hand holding a spoon is stirring coffee.

You see him, and you cannot tell if his bachelorhood is thirty years, or will be... You hear the birds, and there is a hint of rain in the air. There the wet wash blows and kicks by an apple tree.

He was getting full of voices, squeaks, house-thumps (he called them) the noises of things without the things themselves.

Silence and coffee, dust and dead insects, and the way the floorboards run. Not to mention the setting of the sun, that glare of gold on dirty windows.

Or, to mention the moon, and then it is night, with its certain starvation; a need for coffee and music. Which is to wonder which muscle will move first. To be quiet in darkness, until he moves. To move after the desire has passed.

Or, does the heart hunger after cheese, now?

Overhead, the moon. His shadow rides the fore, unhurt by stone, thorn, or the cold slime of the damp earth.

He could have been a Man of Sorrows, at meditation's hour, projecting through his agency such powers as creation's inventory from the seats of primal cause...

Or, he could have been a poet, or a lover; one who intensely sings, with blood as thick as ketchup, and a great boot of a heart, which can thump up the stairs of the breast like a madman with passion's delicate rose...

He was a stingy man, pinchy with cold. With a heart like a

white fist clenched, knuckles and tendons taut. As if he *would* live, even though that white fist of a heart clenched his breast like an overcoat against his living.

He would have his coffee among voices, it was his lot to hear them. He, himself, was squeaking with a continuous flow of sounds. He was haunted, as if he were an empty house; all came and went as they pleased.

A certain train of chords, pleasing. He wondered if, after all, he was not a musician?

Until a certain train of philosophic debates placed him among the thinkers of the world.

Or, should he have placed his hope upon a certain lyricism that wounded his spirit with beauty? A feeling that one is better than oneself...he could, if he wished...but, he is content knowing he could, because all is folly, absurd...

And now his voices. A cup of coffee. A cigarette.

And he had fussy little self-habits. Nervous tics, small habitual movements that somehow seemed right.

There were many little things he had to do. His attention was constantly splintered.

The ticking of clocks, especially small ones, watches, caused him to itch...yes, positively, he had to scratch. He had to blink, or good fortune would pass him by...at least, ill fortune would find him. So that avoiding ill fortune was enough in itself for one of meagre hope to consider good fortune. Let ill fortune avoid him long enough and, perhaps, he would go on to better things.

Meagre hope? Hope was a species that would eat itself out of house and home. From the tiny food of a pleasant moment, hope bred itself like the fruit fly. Until he was soggy with ill-fed flies. Indeed, heavily leadened, as if he were an insect morgue.

Under the toxic affect of dead hope, as it decomposed, he was likely to die. Which meant he would burst like a match into flame, briefly and most convincingly, but really, most charmingly, rising to reckless wit and devil-may-care. Guided only by the fool's star, the star of idiot's luck.

When he woke up, which wasn't likely (why should he presume?)...well, say he did (which is dangerous, he may be signing his own death warrant)...he would not speak of it except to say (in doing so) he realized that later he would return there for the same purpose. Which is the precise use of the bed. Well, let that be...

We come now to his abilities: He heard knocking, when no one knocked. He heard footsteps that were without feet. He accepted these things.

He was, also, stroked, poked and tickled by lascivious hands when he was quite alone. He assumed them to be lascivious, finding no other motive for their incessant exploration. On the other hand, they left him with no feeling except itching. How many hands he could not tell. Hands of a child, hands of an elderly woman? The point is being made, that on a steady diet of coffee, benzedrine and cigarettes until his fingers were brown with smoke, it was no wonder that he heard voices. Well, you see, his parents were gone; also, his siblings and pets.

Bread and wool. Or, I might have said, porridge and crusts of bread, magic foods; mother goods or *goose*. A fondness for toads. A special love for monsters. He could not tell his perverseness from his love. In fact, he did not love. He just tried to get along.

He served himself tea in bed. He waited on himself like a servant, as he cried, please don't treat me like a guest, I can get my own tea. And while I'm about it, would you like some? And then the process in reverse. Or was it reverse? But then he so rarely saw himself, it was hard for him to restrain his joy. There seemed no end to the things he was willing to do to make himself comfortable. Having only one bed, he slept on the floor. He refused his meagre tea in the name of himself. And still he was lonely.

Because he must die, but wasn't dead yet; which is to say because he had run through a fortune and had but one dollar left, still, he had a dollar which he could spend with complete freedom, because his fortune was already spent.

And still, there he was again, scratching...

So, between the nightmare and the lucid moment, let us imagine he must kill the thing he loves.

He had visions earlier, while in medical school, of Professor Flower's face, grey and grave, in his crotch as he passed wind. And violins oozing like maple syrup on the same Professor's grey head as the good Professor explained the function of bile.

He imagined violins plucked into giggles around Professor Flower's head, and the Professor enraged, trying to swat them like a man attacking butterflies.

Now, as the moon is his witness, he must put an end to the thing he loves.

Why?

Love is arbitrary, and the thing is dangerous.

What is it?

It is the very Professor who was father's teacher playing a violin upstairs. It sounds so like the quarreling of angels with its mosquito shrills, hinges of rust and chirping mice... Whilst, in fact, a white moon-fleshed corpse waits to be amputated from the universe.

Father is trying to remember whether he was taught medicine or music. If music, he shall play boom-boom on his drum. If not, he shall not play boom-boom. And yet, now he must, because the thought teases. Yes he will, on the breast of the corpse. Yes, he will play boom-boom, and pretend the corpse's heart is beating. Won't that be fun? No playing, you sonofabitch!

And he is right, because he must amputate the corpse from the universe. It must cease to be, whether alive or dead. Such a thing must never be. It must never have been and it must never come into being. And all future beyond future must recognise this absence.

Still, the violin heard upstairs makes father question his medical background as regards a possible musical one.

And suddenly father breaks out in beautiful soprano from his bass throat. And, so moved is he by this lyricism of his flesh, that his hoarse bass comes back, screaming, I'm musical, I'm musical! But then hearing the mechanical roar of his usual voice, he is drawn back to medicine, and the problem at hand, the death of his Professor.

The hell with the already dead! What kind of Doctor am I anyway, that I have to treat the dead? An undertaker? A necrophile?

It is the living that must be killed, not the dead. It is impossible to kill the dead. They are immuned to dying. There is nothing under the moon that will kill the dead, except those powers that restore life. In that case, one might kill them again. But enough of that.

There is now the question of the Professor upstairs. If I want to kill, it is he who can be killed out of life.

But why must I kill him? I am not sure. But then, if I do kill him, I shall have done it. Whatever reason I come to, still, he must die by my hand. In other words, it must be done. I shall have a multitude of reasons to fit all occasions. But what good will the reasons and excuses be if I haven't killed him? That is putting the mind to work for nothing, it's wasteful.

Father was now beyond a chance of hesitation, like the reasons that the good Professor didn't want to die; and who was he to take another's life without his permission; or even with it?

If I will kill him, I will.

Therefore, the violin splintered as father asked the vital question, did you or did you not teach me medicine? Or, did you or did you not teach me music?

The Professor answers as he dies, I taught you home economics.

With which father beats the dead Flower more soundly than he would have, with rage and frustration at learning how wrongly his life has been spent.

Let us not talk of father for a moment. And let us not imagine that he kills the thing he loves. Let us in our minds amputate him from the universe...

The Courtship

Father did not die. He went to a party and found love.

Old Papa Plume, a rather dishevelled flower, took father to Miss John Mary Wimp's dinner party.

Miss John Mary Wimp curtseyed.

The guests were arriving: The Duke of Maypole, Madam Pastridge, Colonel Muff, Corporal Jasmine, General Moon, and Papa Plume with somebody's daughter, George. (So father seemed at the time.)

Miss Wimp said, would you all like a cocktail? At which, with panic and stampede, they screamed, yes, yes, yes, three jeers for John!

Miss Wimp served rooster plumes, which they chewed, and screamed again, hip, hip, hurray, jolly good awful time!

Corporal Jasmine whispered in Miss Wimp's ear, you've got an awfully pretty ass, I bet ya have a time in the latrine.

Come on, everybody, let's sit down to supper, Miss Wimp yelled. At which a terrible panic began. The guests ran all through the house, screaming, where's it at! I got it! Where? Where? Help, help, I'm starving!

And then Miss Wimp said, in the garage, we'll eat engine sludge.

And so, like a terrible hurricane, like naughty children, they rushed into the garage and ate up the automobile and the chauffeur.

No, no, Miss Wimp said, we're going to have sewer soup with rectum mustard and snot greens. Up through the servant's entrance, through the windows, crying, help! they ran to the dining room, talking rapidly and frothing, fainting and farting.

Soon servants were bringing hot bowls of orange peels and coffee grounds, and steaming old newspapers and delicious broken bottles.

The Duke of The Evening Mist began to make eyes at Papa Plume. Corporal Jasmine began to spoon with General Moon, as Colonel Muff was making out with Madam Pastridge.

And now Miss Wimp was serving wine. Would anyone like some wine? she asked.

And they all began to whine, I want some, oh, please, I want some, me, me ... And they began to hit Miss Wimp on her head with their wine glasses.

After the meal was over they all had some dysentery liqueur.

Papa Plume began to play the violent, accompanied by General Moon's organ. And Corporal Jasmine brought out his English Hound. The Duke of Ambrey began to play with his bum.

Meanwhile, Miss Wimp began to scream with her lovely tenor. They asked for an encore, and Miss Wimp began to curse. They asked for more, and she began to fart.

Anybody for a nightcap? Miss Wimp finally asked.

Her guests began to shout, I want one, I want one, me too, oh, please let me have one...

So Miss Wimp brought out something made of wool and flowers, with veils and brims and crowns, called *Nocturne Chapeau.*

As she was trying to serve it they rushed her, crying, I want mine, it's free, it's mine, give it here!

Who wants some coffee? Miss Wimp asked. And then everyone began screaming at the top of his lungs, I want it, I want it, I want it, I'd murder for it, I'd kill you for being so cruel as to offer it without giving it o'er...

Finally Miss Wimp was curtseying goodnight, and her guests were leaving. She was saying, goodnight all, and please come again. And with that, they all rushed back in, screaming, I want to come again. Here I am. I'm here. I've come again!

And then they began to rush all over the house, stampeding with panic. Screaming, help! help!

And that night in bed father was badly eaten by a woman's buttocks.

The woman had gotten into his mind, kissing the lobes of his brain, spreading madness and tenderness. He had often seen her in the streets and in the woods. She had the hands of a healer. And now she would play mud-pie with his brain.

She had the eyes that *I know* will understand...

And so the next day father went to see Miss Wimp.

George Gulping, get that thing out of here, get that thing out of here this minute, screamed Miss Wimp.

But, Miss Wimp...

I don't care, I don't care what it is, get it out of here!

But, Miss Wimp, it's me...

I don't care, she screamed, take it out of here.

But it's my physical being, my material presence. It's me, Me, ME!, roared father.

Well, it's a terrible sight, a terrible burden for the floors, which are sagging. It has to go, even if it is you. Why, look how your khakis bulge like sausage skins, glistening with the immense wealth of your flesh. And the rich surplus of oil that slicks along the puffed roses of your cheeks.

I cannot help it if my appetite far exceeds my expenditures, and lays like snug burghers along my ribs.

Well, I won't have it, screamed Miss Wimp, I can't stand your whining, your whimpers, the suckle noise of your terrible lips when you dream at night, that great woman's chest of yours bloated and glimmering with heroic pearls of sweat.

Please, Miss Wimp, all of this excitement and exertion has brought up from the depths of my resolve to suffer the pangs of hunger an overwhelming desire for bread and butter, tumble tatter, sherbets of several colors, clover honey, beef stew with roast pork, bacon and eggs topped with lemon cream and granulated sugar, and Mary Better's prize pickles with a dab of cotton candy, and perhaps, a leg of lamb thrown in...

Get out, get out, or I'll call the police. The dam is broken!

Okay, Miss Wimp, I'm going down to Dud & Wylly's ham-and-egg joint.

Go then, just go. Where you go I don't care. Just that you go.

And, feeling that he had made an impression on Miss Wimp, he again visited her. And to his delight and surprise, she served him coffee.

Miss Wimp remarked, on seeing the pink smile on the back of father's neck, would you like some boiling coffee down your back?

No, indeed, father smiled.

Would you like me to throw a cup of coffee in your face?

What's all this with putting hot coffee on me, Miss Wimp? father inquired.

I find you most complacent, you bourgeois cop.

I am not an officer of law enforcement. I am a peek-a-boo man with plumbing in my belly, full of plums and grubs.

Get out! Get out! cried Miss Wimp, your body is too big for your suit, and I can smell your bowels, which are beginning to move. You've soiled yourself!

Oh, what's all this? Stop teasing and kiss my mouth.

Oh no, not that. Your food is coming up, you smell like garbage. Your head looks like a pink condom.

Didn't you send me a note saying your husband would be out, and would I be so kind as to come up and make love to you?

Would you like a hot cup of coffee in your face?

No, said father.

Would you like it down your neck?

No, said father ...

Let me describe father as a fat dirty bag of guts. Let me call him by his obscure name, Olop.

Father has now found my mother. And this is their love and the end of it: Once a dirty fat bag of guts, Olop, was in love with a great animal-fat goddess, Miss Wimp.

Father, or Olop, was standing on a balcony overlooking oblivion, while Miss Wimp was combing out her bristles.

Oh, Miss Wimp, you are like a goddess.

And you, Miss Wimp said, are my angel-knight, who has come to rob me away from boredom.

A piece of father's stomach was hanging out over the top of his pants.

Oh, Miss Wimp, you are my best girl. (You are a girl, aren't you?) Oh, Miss Wimp, I want to molest you. May I molest your head with my lips?

Come to me, squealed Miss Wimp. Your lips are like two pink worms full of human dead.

I love you, love you, Miss Wimp, oh, ugh, Miss Wimp, my dearest, my love.

If you touch me there again I shall scream, screamed Miss Wimp. And she screeched, you're a lot of fun.

You're very nice, roared father.

You're swell, yelled Miss Wimp.

Father was barking, I adore you, I adore you, bow-wow, woof, woof.

Get away from me, you mad dog, meowed Miss Wimp.

Now father was foaming at the mouth, and baring his teeth.

Call The Humane Society, yelped Miss Wimp.

Father leapt on Miss Wimp.

Miss Wimp began to scream, ouch, and, oh, and, oh, indeed, and, goodness, is this real?

Father was panting, and whispering at her ear, dearest, oh, my pretty woman, my great log lassie, my suet fancy...

Oh, I do love you, my fat creature, Miss Wimp whimpered, you are all that I shall ever want.

She began to pet his head. He began to lick her hand. She began to rub his back. He began to wag his tail. She began to scratch his ears. He began to whine, yummy. Suddenly, he leapt at her throat.

She began to scream, you dirty pig, you're a lot of fun.

He roared, I want all the mineral rights, all the copyrights, I want to patent my love, I want to stake a claim.

Drive your stake, she screamed, because you're a lot of fun!

The Marriage

Miss Wimp and George Gulping in Circus X. I am born. The child is Fuzzy Ann.

Shall I tell you secrets about my parents?

My father is a doctor. No, he is a General. Yes, and a doctor, too. On weekends he is a general, and all during the week a doctor.

He is a poet.

Let me talk about their sex...

I should begin: Why we lost the war, and why we had still to lose it.

As a child I was Private Fuzzy Ann, General Gulping's man, attached to the household of the General. Heir apparent by the line of my father.

My mother was a man. One of those rare cases of a rooster laying an egg. A secret kept with the aid of disguise; known only to the family, family retainers, their families, friends; written of at length in many medical journals. But, in fact, kept secret with the other fact, that my father, the General, was a woman.

My title of Private, honorary, at best.

And so I am to do a man's task. I am a soldier. My duty entails being attached to the General's household; so that things are no different, until I wonder if there is a war. If there is a war, it is going badly, because father always makes mistakes. I can say with all due respect, anything he puts his hand to will eventually end in tears. That he will be brought, all tangled in maps and telephone cords, to his room, weeping and sighing, and put to bed without supper.

With despair, so touching it is true, as he picks his nose with abandonment, asking why it is he and not the enemy General who must be disgraced by starvation; and couldn't he have a cookie or two, or perhaps a leg of lamb to tide him over until morning? Until mother must resort to slapping and hissing at father who, in the meantime, has wet his khakis, not to mention his shirt front with his slobber and tears; his nervous ear-cleaning and ass-scratching, until he must be slapped nearly unconscious and placed in a restraining sheet.

It is very interesting, the inside life of a great man, which my father is, as is seen in the great triumphs of the battlefield which end in routs, scheduled to bring his men home in time for lunch. Which the enemy are prone to call disorderly retreats. And which, on consideration, might well be characterized as men running for their lives to lunch. Either running from bullets, or running to lunch, or both, which would be a great stratagem in its accomplishment, in that movement can at its beginning and at its end, in two places, its extremes, do a double service... Or am I swayed by the love of father, which I deny for the sake of objectivity. Which is to say, I love no one, nor hate; not judgement nor conclusion. I watch. I wait. I understand.

And then, father hiding in the attic among cobwebs, in the dust. Introspective, and afraid to come down, as it were, into life. The ceilings discolored from the General's urination.

He is heard talking to the mice, who also live in the attic.

We shout up occasionally, are you alive, sir?

And then father sighs down, alive, but more nearly dead. But really dead, and just a little alive. On the percentage basis, and for simplicity, I think dead is the word.

And then we might say, oh, then roast pork and black-eyed peas couldn't interest you?

And then he is heard to be moving, as he cries, out of my way if you value your lives. I shall eat you out of house and home. My appetite is fairly big, my dangerous foes.

Mother quickly boards up the attic entrance, from which father breaks through with all introspection forgotten, crying, hi ya, Miss Wimp. And right down to the kitchen he goes.

And very soon mother and father are on the kitchen floor, the roast sliding and they're fighting for it.

Meanwhile, the enemy is charging, and the house is on fire, and father has wet his khakis. And all is being lost, until finally all is lost, and father must be retired to his room.

And then the enemy is approaching, father is running up and down the stairs, screaming to his wife, I can't find my medals. John Mary, my medals, my medals!

I'm trying to feed Fuzzy Ann, and you're scaring her with all that commotion.

You would like to have me found out without my medals, oh horrible woman who commands respect for being a General's wife.

If you love me, she said, you will let me feed the fruit of our love. She's half crazy with the fires of war, which you continually bring into the house; tossing and turning all night. Stratagems until I'm half crazy with the blood-lust. And now, at half-past ten in the morning, you have invited the enemy to lay siege to our home, just as I am attempting the dangerous and delicate job of feeding our half-mad daughter.

What shall I do? I've set the world on fire. I've kindled hatred into quite a blaze. Only fire will quell fire. Shall I turn on my tears to settle it? I haven't cried since I cried last. At the time, vowing never to indulge the histrionics of grief again. I was fifteen. No one cared. To have brought out my despair, and to have had it ignored, tended only to rob the small value that hidden grief may have. May have! Why, it's the most valuable thing in the world. It is, indeed, the only thing we really have. No, I will not weep. No, I will not wet fires I have started with tears, nor beg the enemy from their course.

You are a hard man and a weakling. The hard man is a weakling. His hardness is only a rigidity caused by fear. His hardness is an eggshell, wherein his slimy guts tremble.

Enough. My medals, they will save the day. If hung right, a bullet, aimed at my heart hits a medal, appropriately hung, is deflected. My bravery serves to protect me.

Well, do for Fuzzy Ann's sake go into the yard and fight. I don't want them tramping up the house with muddy feet. Those horrible skirmishes in the hall. Fuzzy Ann awakes screaming in the night, bullets flying over her crib. Assassins coming in and out of her window...

No one is safe, my dear John Mary. As for myself, I shall be in the den with a map, or some property befitting the occasion.

On Monday life shall be different. Father home from battle, the enemy beaten back for a time. Mother, unnerved. Father preparing to meet his patients. Circus X... Monday, mother nervous, Olop getting closer. She began to bathe Fuzzy Ann, scrubbing her cartilage flowers and her head stem. Over and over again she bathed Fuzzy Ann, until she was red and shiny.

Miss Wimp brewed coffee, and then threw it out and brewed more. She was nervous, and her whole body stuttered with repetitions.

Father said, damn you, will you stop washing me? I'm not a child.

Aren't you? she replied, then who are you? I thought *she* was Mr. Gulping, my husband.

No, no, my dear, *that's* Fuzzy Ann. I am the husband.

Then who is Olop, the one who's scaring me shitless? she asked.

Will you tie my tie? father asked.

Well, who is he? she asked.

How in hell should I know or care? screamed father.

But I'm afraid, darling. Do you want me to be afraid? I might injure the child.

Just try it, all I say is, just try it, he roared, but I'm going to be late for the office if you don't tie my tie, brush my teeth, eat my breakfast, take my bus, greet my patients, examine them, touch them, soothe them...

Perhaps father is not a doctor. But he is in his office trying to be one.

At his office, a man in the mirror spoke to father, you are fat.

Yes, he answered, I am very fat; obese. I am *fat* is quite precise. But then, so are you, you in the mirror.

That is quite so, said the image in the mirror. Yes, quite the fat fellow. We are both fat people.

We are not people, smirked father. Only I am people, only I am fat. You are merely an image.

Who's the image?

You are. You only do what I do. I am the original Doctor Gulping.

Who is?

Look, I am doing this and that, wagging my tongue, and crossing my eyes...

So am I!

Enough, cried father. And he slouched down in his Morris chair. And adjusting his jowls, his guts, his gums, he slept.

He awoke as light as smoke. As fair and foolish as the blossom and the maiden.

He remembers the good Doctor Gulping. The clumsy, bear-like, horrible Doctor Gulping. That monstrous animal with hair in its nostrils and ears. That bushy-headed, bespectacled, paunchy, disgusting, I-wouldn't-let-him-touch-me-if-I-were-dying old man...

Father, as fine as mist floated over city and forest... Father as fine as mist floated through the mind of Doctor Gulping.

His image in the mirror sat hunched in the meditation of sleep, as did the real Doctor Gulping, in his real Morris chair, in his real office. While his real patients waited in his real waiting room, cursing real curses.

Now father thickened into ocean water; into dark depths and sunny shallows; fish pierced, thick, unmoving, swaying, slow translucent; fat...

Meanwhile, his patients are pressing at the door, coughing and moaning. Belching and sighing. Complaining. Angry with pain. Enraged by neglect. Martyred. Killed. Retching. Praying. Pressing.

The door began to give way, as if an ocean of wax were pressing; entering, tearing, gushing. The door splintered. The wall broken. The portrait of grandfather flung to the floor, its glass broken, its mustaches unperturbed; Doctor Gulping's degree, certificate, high school diploma, Home-Sweet-Home embroidered motto, barometer, clock and pencil sharpener.

The telephone rang. He picked it up. His wife was screaming

in her most pleasant shout, don't forget the shopping list. My hat at Froggie's. The fitting for my dress. To walk the dog. To be home in time for supper. To prepare it. To serve it to me in my bed. To pamper me to death.

Father said, not now, dear.

She roared, if not now, when? When, if not now? If not now, when? When?

Some other time, darling, I'm busy.

And so father dropped back to sleep. *It's easier that way.*

But now the mirror was broken. Yes, Doctor Gulping lay in splinters around father's feet. Along with grandfather's portrait, the whiskers still unruffled, the degree, certificate, high school diploma, Home-Sweet-Home motto, barometer, clock and pencil sharpener...

Doctor Gulping knows who he is. His wife is waiting. Father has forgotten who he is. His wife is screaming.

And then father starts anew. Retiring to write scientific papers, or poems.

Miss John Mary Wimp and Doctor George Gulping and their daughter, Fuzzy Ann, and their handyman Alfred, with his wife, Madam Alfred, and their daughter, Alfreda, were quite willing, and ready, too, at all costs, no price too great, to take their beds, their washstands, towels and napkins across the frontier. They will start anew with father, who now remembers who he is. He is happy as he smokes his pipe. And he is writing a paper on his experiments with death.

As he thinks of a new life, he is writing about death.

His daughter, Fuzzy Ann, says, daddy, write about life.

Father roaring, let me alone, or I shall dedicate your life to science. Whereupon, Miss Wimp reproves her husband with, if you must kill, kill Alfreda, she's only the handyman's daughter.

Let me work, screams father, or I shall take everyone with me.

Where are you going, darling?

I shall be driven to suicide by not being allowed to follow my vocation. I shall grow nervous. Can't sleep. Toss all night. Short with my colleagues. Rings under my eyes. Under a great strain. And then, suicide. Leaving tremendous scientific achievements behind me. *He gave his all for his art.*

But, said Miss Wimp, you are not an artist.

But what I do is an art, for its being totally creative.

Yes, but you are a totally uncreative, stupid old man.

That is true. But it doesn't alter the case for regenerative activity, that might, in the course of a few hours, prove the worth of all my days of consuming what others have made. I might very well be able to pin an insect down and cry, see what I have done! I might be able to sum up all of science, without too much effort, by pinning an insect to a board and exclaiming, look, see what I have done!

You might very well. And I applaud your enterprise. And after you do that, you will clean the latrine. Doctor Alfred has made a most worthy try at the job, and has failed, in spite of all encouragement.

But there is nothing to cleaning a latrine, screamed father. And why are you calling the handyman doctor? He is no more a doctor than I am. And I am called doctor, so why in hell shouldn't he be? And after all, why shouldn't he be called doctor? He has as much right to the title as I. Which is not the point at all. Which is the latrine. The household is going to pot under your direction, Miss Wimp. And it sickens me to see the house fall down around our ears. Here I am, trying to improve the world, and you let the house fall around our ears as you wring your hands, whimpering and soliciting my services like a woman of the streets. As for our daughter, Fuzzy Ann, playing with the servants' child, Alfreda, I'll have no more of it. Such democratic slumming is quite out of the question. I will not have the two of them pressing their noses at my study window, as if they were equals. I sometimes wonder if you have any regard for me, the way you allow me to get out of humor just as my work piles up. Knowing as well as I, for all your maidenly modesty, that there are bills to be paid. Yes, pressing needs all around us... Wait a minute, John Mary, dearest...

Father suddenly saw himself in a tree whistling, do re mi. A miniature in feathery splendor.

How splendid, with my skin claws and all, he sighed.

A small voice, becoming louder. A loud voice, becoming even louder. His female self-wife at the door. Fat, holding dustmop, rolling pin, wooden stirring spoon, washrag, dustpan, wishbone. With a faint trace of the Doctor about her chin. Which was fuzzy. Which was unseemly. Which didn't matter anymore.

Father said, calmly, in the face of his household, take the loud-loud to a softer loud, and then, gradually, into a small voice, so we can begin preliminary talks about your latest grievance.

Suddenly he saw all the mice of the house, standing around his wife's feet. Staring, they accuse. And the cat and the dog. The cups and the saucers, spoons and forks. And, clunking up the stairs, the dining room chairs, the living room sofa, the kitchen sink, and grandfather's portrait; the gilt frame walking the stairs, chipping its corners, with grandfather's mustaches stiffly unmoving; his eyes pure, his eyes cruel; inhuman makes them cruel; righteous.

Doctor Gulping put himself together. He is stout. No, he is fat. He is pendulous, with tufts of hair here and there. His belly is a smiling droop, with a mustache and an idiot tongue.

His breasts are maidenly. Decidedly Eve-ish. Young Eve had breasts like father's; lovely doe-noses, pink, sweet noses, doves asleep...etc.

But he had much hair between Eve's breasts. He was wearing striped underpants. He was wearing socks and shoes. He was wearing a shirt and a tie. He had a wen on the right side of his upper neck between his ear and the line of his hair. Nostrils and ears are stuffed with black hair, harmonizing with the black bush of his head. He wears glasses. He has a key chain. A pain in his back. He has a stickpin. A medical practice decaying for lack of interest. He has a stethoscope and ivy growing on his windowsill.

Oh, ganging up? Why not? Sure. The mice and the cupboard. Why not the sink and the ... oh, there you are; and my wife in all her household finery, ugly and old, unlovely and fat, scolding. Oh, and grandfather in a gilt frame, surgeon and scholar, horseman, homespun philosopher, wife-beater, disciplinarian, soldier, statesman, stiff-necked, pinch-arsed, stomach-in, dromedary herdsman, herding liquid fellows in a wasteland. And the parasitic pussy-cat. And the doggie, with its head hungry for my hand to pat it; or, perhaps, it's jaws hungry for my rich throat. The slum-souled mice. The dining room chairs, which which would make splendid firewood.

Now his wife began to say, first in a small voice, and then in a loud voice, and still louder, the rent is due. The cupboard is bare. My stockings are run. The cat's without milk. The dog without bone. The mice without garbage. My hair without pins. My cheeks without rouge.

I'm tired of life, said Doctor Gulping.

But father was not really as tired of life as Doctor Gulping thought he was. And so he lay down, and his household vanished.

He could see himself sleeping. Which was odd, because usually he was inside himself. Odd, too, he was asleep in the arms of a naked woman. Overhead, a palm tree, with a monkey's anus projecting between the leaves.

Father said, I'm tired of life! And he began to run. Through many streets. Through forests. Seasons. Along aqueducts. Jumping canals. Hiding in the rushes. Paddling furiously across the Styx. Panting. Trotting. Galloping. Whuppee!

It began to rain. Sweet the rain! It began to snow. Sweet the snow! Everything began: Snow Rain Flower Tree Child God Fish Fire Form Foot ... Whuppee!

The Soldier

Father was down in the cellar with his staff. Father was leaning over some maps. A corporal had a grey rat he was petting. Captain Mommy was polishing his boots.

The Corporal said, hey General, this rat wants to bite you.

Be a good boy, replied father.

But he wants to bite you, General. He's hungry, screamed the Corporal.

Are you mad? I could have you court-martialed, yelped father.

But, General Gulping, just one little bite. Just a tiny nip no bigger than a rat's jaw, you selfish pig, roared Corporal Jasmine.

Captain Mommy, mommy, whimpered father, please don't let Corporal Jasmine put a rat on me.

Captain Mommy said to Corporal Jasmine, you know better than to tease the General. You're in the army, and we're under fire. The General's studying maps and plans. The war depends on him. And then a silly little Corporal wants to put a rat on the great General. I can hardly believe this is true. Now tell the General you're sorry. Go ahead...

But this rat's hungry. He said he was, screamed the Corporal.

General, the Captain implored, how about it, just one little bite, to quiet the Corporal.

No, no, cried father, beginning to go into a tantrum.

The Corporal was saying to the rat, sic 'im, go on, sic 'im.

The rat was baring its teeth. Father was screaming, Mommy, mommy, Captain Mommy, quickly, it's going to bite me.

Captain Mommy, trying to soothe him, there, there, General, the Corporal was just having a little game. It's all right, you can continue the war...easy, General, easy, sweetheart, it's all right.

And Corporal Jasmine said, I was just fooling, this rat wouldn't bite you. He likes you. See, he's wagging his tail.

Father was sobbing. I thought, for a minute, he was going to bite me...sob...

General, Captain Mommy said, before you go back to the war, I wonder if you would kiss my boots. They're so shiny; I wonder if you wouldn't just kiss them?

I will not, said father. A man in my position can't go around kissing the boots of a Captain, even if they are so nice and shiny.

Then Corporal Jasmine said, may this hungry rat bite you?

Father said, I will kiss Captain Mommy's boots if he protects me from the dangerous infection of the rat's bite.

Captain Mommy said, please leave me out of your affairs with the rat. I merely want you, as a personal favor to me, to kiss my shiny boots. I want you to grovel before me, as if I were your superior, while I know you are mine. I would get a particular enjoyment if you would bow down and kiss my boots.

I can't very well, said father, since I went to West Point, and have become a very important person. And this is why I can't allow the rat to bite me, either. I must maintain a certain dignity, because people would say what kind of General is he, letting a rat bite him, and bowing before his Captain's boots to kiss them. (Which are beautiful, I must admit, and do deserve kissing; and which tempt me more than I would like to say.)

Oh, come on, General, Captain Mommy whimpered, who will know, except us? And you can count on us to keep the secret, as long as you pay us a thousand a week. Come on, here in the privacy of this cellar, bow down to my boots, and let the rat bite you...

Well, said father, perhaps I might just peck one of your white gloves. Something quite casual, as if I were stooping to pick up a piece of paper from the floor, and my face brushed against your glove, quite by accident.

No, General, said the Captain, that will not do.

Perhaps I'll blow a kiss to your boots. That'll be quite romantic, yelped father.

No, General, Captain Mommy said, that will not do. You must get on your knees and say, Your Royal Highness, will you permit me to kiss your boots? Nothing else will do.

But I am the General, and you are but a lowly Captain. How dare you even suggest I kiss your boots? Although, again, I admit the prospect of kissing those shiny wonders does seem attractive. I must say again, you have no right expecting your commanding officer to bow before you.

General, General, cried Corporal Jasmine, the rat's sick. He needs food.

The Corporal was holding the famished rat in his hands. He approached the General.

General, let him nibble on your double chin, for only five minutes.

No, no, get that thing out of here.

Please, General, put him inside your shirt, so he can sink his teeth into your lush flesh, implored the Corporal.

Mommy, mommy, do something with this incorrigible boy, crooned father.

I'm quits, said Captain Mommy. What kind of General are you, anyway, that you can't do a Captain a personal favor? If you had kissed my boots, you would now be busily at your maps, conducting the war. But, as it is now, well, General, you can plainly see, you have no friends. You might be able to win the rat over by giving him a meal, but as for me, if you kissed my boots now, it would only seem as if you were trying to make me feel good, and that wouldn't do at all, because I've a very large ego, and when a General kisses my boots I like to feel he's doing it only because my un-advertised importance demands it.

Father whimpered, if I let the rat chew on the back of my neck for ten minutes, will you, Corporal Jasmine, be nice to me until the end of the war?

Oh, no, the Corporal said, now it's too late. Now the rat knows exactly what sort of person you are.

Please, begged father, please let me put the rat inside my clothes.

Unh, unh, said the Corporal, if the rat were dying... No siree, the rat doesn't want that kind of gift.

Won't either of you let me do anything for you? pleaded father. Look, I'll cut my hand and feed the rat some blood to awaken his appetite. Captain, I'll not only kiss your boots, I'll kiss your ass; and you can pass wind if you want to. Oh, but please let me mortify myself.

Listen, General, said Captain Mommy, we'll serve you in our official capacities, fair enough; but, as to liking you, well, that is quite another thing. And, I don't mind telling you when we're in contact with the troops again, it shall make the rounds that you refused to kiss my boots, and refused to feed a hungry rat. How do you think it'll sound to the mothers back home, that you refused to let a rat bite you? And how do you think the officers under you will feel when they find out that you wouldn't kiss my shiny boots? And the fact that all through the battle I did nothing else but shine them, hoping the General would notice and bow down before me and kiss my boots to distraction.

Look, said father, as he lifted some soggy sewerage from the floor, I'm pouring filth on the General. I'm turning him into a regular K.P. fellow.

The Corporal screamed, General, you are beginning to smell! You are basically foul, despite all your medals to the contrary.

The General, interjected Captain Mommy, is not the fellow I should like to be wrecked on a desert island with.

Why doesn't the General inspire love? pleaded father.

He might inspire pity, yet, he is too disgusting. His weakness is not pitiable. It makes one angry. One wishes to hurt. Even, to ruin the shine on one's boots with the General's blood. If you get what I mean, General, said Captain Mommy.

Yes, yes, screamed father. One wishes to destroy by great pain an awkward situation that has no dignity, like a fat General full of medals.

General, roared Captain Jasmine, the rat has just fainted!

Oh, my, he must be all tuckered out, murmured father, with womanly concern.

And now, General, commanded Captain Mommy, I would like to hit you on the head with a brick; perhaps pull all your hair out.

Oh yes, you must do something terrible to me, I understand. It all stems from the fact that I didn't stoop and kiss your lovable boots; and then, when I was ready to, I had lost the right to.

I'm going to kill you, General, said Captain Mommy.

Please do not hurt a hair on my head, cried father.

I'm going to kill all that digestive plumbing that pushes out the front of your uniform, whined Captain Mommy.

Corporal Jasmine, screamed father, I order you to kill Captain Mommy before I can say Jack and the Beanstalk!

If you will comfort the rat, sway it in your arms and sing to it, replied Corporal Jasmine.

Of course, give me the little fellow! There, there, you dirty rat, you louse-infested, disease-carrying pest. ...*When the wind blows...* Now what's the matter wid da itty bitty shit-stained rodent? crooned father.

Now hurry up, Corporal Jasmine, kill Captain Mommy before I can say Jack and the Beanstalk.

Don't you dare touch me. And if you get a speck of dirt on my handsome footwear...if you mar the shine, even so much as by trying to spruce up by looking in the mirror-effect of these lovely and most awe-inspiring, these beautiful examples of artistic achievement, these art treasures of lovable leather; if you dare, I shall most certainly stamp them with impatience at your philistine attitude towards this century's greatest cultural achievement, said Captain Mommy.

Oh, dear, screamed father, I think I love this rat! I think I must kiss it, or forever thirst for its lips.

Now wait, General, roared the Corporal, it's only a child. Sure, I understand that in times of war social customs get out of joint, and that one may be dead tomorrow and all; but you're far too ugly to engage this animal in the complications of housekeeping. Which means, getting the children off to school, picking you up at the station, dodging the exterminator, trying to look pretty for you, and at the same time keeping contact with other rats. In fact, living two lives, one in the living room, and one in the walls.

Of course, you're right, whimpered father, I could only bring misery to my little bride. And, incidentally, I think this rat's a male, anyway. I see now that it would never work out.

Corporal Jasmine said, and now I'll kill Captain Mommy.

Before you do, said Captain Mommy, I should like to make a verbal will, that on the event of my death, will be shouted throughout the world: I, Captain Mommy, being of sound mind and body, wearing the most exquisite boots (they really are!) …having entered the military world for the sole purpose of securing the right to wear cavalry boots without people saying, as they do of civilians, that he is putting on airs; and having spent my entire career in the polishing of same, feel now loath to be parted from such glistening leather. (Indeed, more bright than sunshine, which may be the exaggeration that love exacts.) Therefore, I consign all pensions, or monies resulting from the activities which make me the recipient of such monies, etc., to the care and maintenance of said glorious, almost unholy in their unnatural beauty, boots. Also, I stipulate that they be exhibited in the Royal London Museum, the Metropolitan of New York, and the Louvre of Paris; and that only high persons view these precious and most darling boots in the private offices of the museum directors. And that, under no condition shall they be used as footwear, even if it is raining. But that, on the occasion of a coronation, they be present, and be carried on a red pillow, signifying their importance, to any state they visit. And that they be referred to as *Their Highness'*. And, that the Queen of England pose with them on her lap. And, that the President of the United States address odes to these boots over the radio. And, further, that, even in the event of my untimely death, they not be removed from my feet. Signed (verbally), Captain Mommy.

Very commendable, Captain. Very fine; you're a true soldier, sighed father, as he collapsed.

Father in half-state: The mice are singing hymns, like good country folk. Fleas feasting, dinner in fur. And all about the country sleeps.

Soldiers die. Yes, the soldier's wife is watching the moon by the window in her daughter's room. The child in her crib, pearly with sweat, snores, angel-fallen on a rock-bed of linen.

Now the jaw of the graveyard, thick with teeth. Now the mammary hills. Now the sperm dot of the moon. Now time and time and time... Back, back before dying there is... Yes, I remember quite as well, as well, as well... And before that, and before that. Which is time, time before...

A white cup and its saucer. Cauliflower for dinner.

William is crying, her doll is full of maggots. Do comfort her, George.

I pour the coffee, love. Two flats (you think of my breasts) is that enough? Here is the cream, and stirring, and you look upon me. My hair is ugly; and the wrinkle? Yes, the wrinkle is coming into my face. You, yourself, are thickening in the middle.

I smile. You stir. And, after all... And hear the child. It cries. It is made of us.

Cauliflower for dinner with ham steaks, pickles and milk, and a touch of Alfred in your eyes because I am ugly. Well, I don't pretend to compete.

Now, the trumpets of war, whilst you are growing fat. Diplomats talk. The fires begin, kindled by small words, raging out of hand between men.

Soon I heard the soldiers going forth. William crying, her doll full of maggots.

Last meal: cauliflower, and you will write, George? Ham steaks, come back to us safe. Have I packed everything? Tuxedo, your straw hat, dancing slippers, the chicken sandwich, the love letters of Alfred, your tuxedo... Kiss me, then, George, and go. Kiss William, and her doll. Yes, each maggot. Summon the mice of the house, and kiss each in turn on its whiskers.

At first, when I heard you were dead, I knew you were dead.

And then I said, oh, no, George looks dead, but he's not dead. No, George has looked dead for years. The dinner bell made a Lazarus of him. Or, I bare myself naked to him, and he is like a thousand monkeys in my tree. Here in the moonlight, George is not dead.

William is snoring.

Someplace George thinks, under the moon, of Alfred...

Breakfast, coffee and cauliflower. William still crying. The neighbor's wife scolding her child. The child crying. A door slamming. George, cut your cauliflower in smaller pieces. William, stop crying and pluck the maggots out. I can't find them, and a new burst of tears. Until I am half out of my wits. You'll be late for the office, George.

I cannot believe George would die. Only yesterday a letter: Dear John Mary, I want a divorce. Alfred and I are living together, and are happy. Please send my hair lotion and my tweezers. Regards to William, George.

Notes from the house of the injured. First day's observation:

And what do you think of the dead, Nurse Milly?

Oh, they're fine; great fellows they are.

And the child, William, lying some forty years...?

She's a great one, she is; like all them lazy dignitaries of Egypt, Denmark, Hong Kong...they're a great bunch, just full of fun and worms.

And, Nurse Milly, what of wife John Mary and husband George Gulping and their daughter William, and her puppy dog Johnson, and its flies and their offspring who remain nameless?

They're all very much of another time, I fear. And I am not acquainted with their household, where the puppy dog, Johnson, at my approach lifted his upper lip to show me his eye-teeth. Or did he wag his waggy? And the wife, John Mary Wimp, said, sorry, we don't need any…and I went home and brooded that I would never make a successful salesman. And all that sort of nonsense, of which I know nothing.

Oh, let's talk about the dead, Nurse Milly.

Oh, yes, let's. If we don't, they'll talk about us.

Well, Nurse Milly, what do you think of the dead?

Let me think; certainly I must think something of the dead. Let me see…oh, yes, they're a fine bunch, great fellows they are.

Indeed, Nurse, and are you not awestruck at their number?

Yes, I never did like crowds. That murmur, that subdued agitation, that restless and dangerous weight…

Ah, yes, but the dead sleep and do not wander. And, if they do, they are without substance, they come only as ideas, visions … And they are spooky, aren't they, sir?

Yes, Nurse Milly, they are a troublesome lot of beggars.

Yes, they are, so let's stop talking about them right this minute, or I shall scream a duet.

Second day's observation: Doctor Flower, followed by Nurse Milly, approached my bed and said, hello. How do you feel? I'm Doctor Flower.

Nurse Milly: Is the great poet dead?

Flower: No.

Milly: Is he in pain?

Flower: Great pain for a great poet.

Milly: Does the earth hunger to eat back its constipation?

Flower: Do I know, you stupid thing?

Milly: You sonofabitch!

Flower: For the sake of the Goose, keep your temper leashed.

Nurse Milly to me: Where does it hurt, sir?

Goose: My ankle, I think it's sprained.

Flower to me: You're dying of old age. Your organs are dry like stones. There has been wine and laughter, fame and love, scandal and fortune...

Goose: Oh, yes, I'm a big shot.

Milly: May I have your autograph, sir?

Goose: Have a fingerprint. Or, would you like a urine sample?

Flower: Are you comfortable, Dr. Goose?

Goose: My hair hurts.

Flower: How can your hair hurt?

Goose: I'm only trying to cooperate.

Milly to Flower: Maybe you ought to perform a mercy killing.

Flower: Why, idiot?

Milly: To save the great poet the pain of death.

Goose: Don't you dare touch a hair of my head.

Flower: It is true, sir, that the funeral arrangements are made, and great crowds are waiting to wave you to the grave.

Goose: Well, I want to write a swan song first.

Milly (screams): Oh, a blood sonnet, sir!

I said: A urine sonnet. Why not?

Milly: Oh, darling, you're wonderful!

Goose: There are many things that must be said before you draw the sheet o'er a man like a swan's down of snow, when the flesh can sing no more... Oh, my friends, oh, my beloved, hear the young girl's heart through an old man's throat; for, his songs are young, though the swan is dying...

Milly: Oh, we melt like wax in the flame of your tongue.

Goose: Let ravens black, bats and mourning women follow. Let leashed toads and buzzing clouds of maternal flies there follow on the funeral box. Put the Taj Mahal, Eiffel Tower, St. Paul's and the Empire State Building on the road to the funeral pit. Have crazy girls laughing. Have madmen beseech the moon as I pass by. Let all confetti fall. And, as I descend, let all descend by suicide...

Milly (screams): Oh, yes, I'll cut my throat now if you wish it. May I jump on your body and stomp on the red grapes of your flesh? Oh, let me do something horrible. Like poking the fawn's eye with a switchblade knife. Perhaps I could piss on you?

Flower to Milly: Do not be carried away by this old fool's talk. I've never held with poets. Their cork-lined ivory towers, and their holier-than-thou anachronistic shepherd song in our modern city of steel. As if satyr and angel, prophetic supermen. You need a sedative, Nurse.

Milly: No, no, what he says is so. Dr. Goose is a real swan. Keeper of the lucid mystery, clear as the black pool of midnight, where the swan glides, like a drift of snow in the forest of the night...

Goose: Mount the funeral coach with woman's ass. Line the coffin with woman's breast. Let the air attending on the scene be filled with woman's scream. And let the horses wear panties on their heads. Let roses and stockings of silk be cast before the horses. Let brides desert their grooms for the stink of death.

Flower: Enough of the Goose playing swan. Actually, you're an old bum with a touch of dysentery.

Milly: He is not! He's better than you are.

Flower (leaves): I'll be back in seven minutes to see how we shall cut you. You need cutting badly.

Milly: I will stay with you, sir. I adore you. I want to kiss your foulest place.

I: Get away, your love is full of teeth.

Milly: Let me kill you!

I: Get away.

Third day's observation: Waiting for the return of Doctor Flower, who wishes to cut me.

Seven minutes before the hour. Today they are going to put frogs down my neck. Why? Because toads are land frogs, you son of a bitch.

And now turtles are beginning to walk in the broad avenue of my heart, where sunbeams have made gold of gore, where the gutters run red in the rosy bladder.

The frogs are hurting my spine with their broad-brimmed mouths.

Quite seriously, if you put another green dignitary down my back I shall sing of love. Which is the hate of whomsoever abideth under the lust cover of the spiritual ascension to the underground mooring of the mushroom, where she sings now that death has angeled the mauve phantom of her boudoir, so that young maidens do behave on the green arse of the hill, and so forth...

Six before the hour. If I can not thread this needle before evil... Evil? And now camels begin to walk...

My pubic hairs are spiders. Madam Spider killed her husband. Oh, dear, can that be me? That celibate webbing...

Five before the hour. Doctor Flower will be here in five minutes; and the frogs, up and down my back. Foolishness, and all manner of jest. I shall open my heart for flowers and laughing children, sunlight and dust. It shall be Springtime. A confetti of laughter, flowers... I want an ice cream cone, and who's that?

Four before the hour. My stomach is nervous. I'm beginning to belch fish bubbles and snowflakes. My leg is jumping with jitterbug. Now my eyes are beginning to blink like jump-rope.

If Doctor Flower doesn't come soon, I shall leap from the window.

Three before the hour. Someone is knocking. Doctor Flower is early. Knock your knuckles off, Harry...

Two before the hour. He's still knocking. Soon he will leave, without knowing how much I wanted to see him. Why am I so perverse?

One minute before the hour. Doctor Flower, the door is locked. I have the key. You are on the outside. My tongue is sticking out in your direction. You must think I'm silly...

Exactly the hour. Doctor Flower has gone away, thinking I don't love him. While, in truth, I adore him beyond measure. If only I told him. But I'm too nervous to be bothered with people. I must attend to the house. I have lots of scratching to do. Lots of twitching to do. Pacing and thinking. I have to look under the bed because I know no one is there. But I must make sure. I can't have Harry Flower saying I'm silly because I know no one is there, while still I know someone might be there. It's like you know Miss Wimp is jumping off the roof. You see her dress ballooning out as she sails downward. You hear her plop. You see the black box pass the window. And yet, you know Miss Wimp is home telling William Ann the story of seventeen lubs. And, sure enough, she is at home telling Tuttle the story of seventeen rattles. And you learn it was William Ann who passed by in a black box. So that someone is probably under the bed right now. And that someone is Miss Wimp.
Hi ya, John Mary.
And now Miss Wimp begins to tell me the story of seventeen

dub-dubs.

Fourth day's observation. They are operating me. Conversation and sensations.

What I said: Don't let that hammer fall! If you dare to let it fall on my foot, Doctor Harry Flower, you shall awake into darkness where nightingales are distant, and from this bright world hushed, Harry. Like Nurse Milly, when the heart is foul with love of a married man; and one is married to him, and really hates him but pretends love.

If you let that hammer fall, Harry, as dark as the moon is in its place, so shall the gates fall away from you like a tiger-pit... Harry! For pity's sake put down that hammer or I'll spit. Harry, for God's sake...

What Harry said: Don't you spit at me. If you dare to offend me with spew I'll bust all the fine bones of your toes. You act like a man who went to sleep, seeing as how the day had passed the moment of its high empty splendor. And now the mosquitos begin to blend the song of blood, quite delicately muted, as to be suggestive of some faint and distant nightingale's cry, and hearing this he awoke in the dark and slapped his own face. Growing angry, he slaps himself again for the hurt. Now he begins to spit. Now he accuses people of hitting his feet with hammers. Now he threatens darkness...the oppressive song of angels.

What I said: Now I plead, Doctor Harry. Before I threatened. Now I plead with you to help me save your life. For if that hammer falls, I shall take your life; just as surely as I shall tell Milly, which is as sure as shit. If you hurt my ankle bone so I can't dance nicely, like I do, I'll set Nurse Milly's alarm clock so it'll ring thirty-three minutes past three. You see if I don't.

What Nurse Milly said: Don't you dare let that hammer fall

before I grab hold of it and help you bring it down. If you don't let me help you hurt him, Harry, you shall awaken into a darkness. This I swear, in the name of all the pebbles in my garden.

What I said: Ow, oh, that hurts! Ow, I see stars! Ow, ow! Oh, what cruelty! Oh, my goodness! Oh, what a cruel joke! Harry, for pity's sake, at least knock off the rest of the foot. It looks silly to leave that tendon with the pinky toe hanging off of it.

What Nurse Milly said: Look into my face, Doctor, I would not want to shoot you in the back. Turn around, Harry. Turn around, sweet Harry.

What Harry said: Turn around, turn around, said she. You fuck yourself. I ain't never turning around so you can shoot me, like you said.

What I said: My feet are hammered off. So what! So my feet are hammered off. So, okay. What about it? All right. So now I ain't got feet. So what should I do, cry? Tear my hair? The hell with it!

What Doctor Flower said: You tell 'em. You tell 'em good.

What I said: Hey Milly, you and Harry are swell guys not to leave a cripple. You'll always stand by me, won't you?... For God's sake, don't let that hammer fall on my head. For the sake of all that's kind and reasonable in the world. For the sake of the birds that sing so sweetly. You heard them, good as I, in the Spring...you know how they sing? That hammer's going to hurt ... Gosh, it hurts. Ow, ow, ow, I see stars... I feel I'm awakening into darkness... Look out! I'm going to spit. And I'm going to tell Nurse Milly on all of you. You just wait till I see Doctor Harry Flower, boy... Oh, look at the stars!

A letter father sent to mother: Dear Miss Wimp, They have cut off my legs. But I fear not, since the bed has legs. And so, when they are out, I explore the house, riding on my bed.

In fact, dear John Mary, I think they have removed my entire body from my soul. I am in a state of amputation. That's it! I infected by body...or, is it my soul?

They have cut off something. Disconnected something. Perhaps the electricity?

I have been amputated. I have lost my true purpose, which was toward the moon! When it is full it makes you feel so good.

My friend, I am deciding whether or not to send you my ear, like the great one did.

They are doing things to my body. I say to them, you may have anything, if only you will leave me alone.

Cut my fingers. That's it, cut off my fingers. Devour them, see if I care! Eat them, eat them!

If the weather continues nice, I shall ride up to mucus point. Which is certainly my nose, which continuously drips. Would they say, now blow? Oh, no, it is not as though I couldn't do that myself. But they have cut my arms off! It is only by special effort, and because I love you truly, that I can write this letter.

If I go to speak they cut my tongue out. Just as I am about to pronounce a difficult syllable, they cut it out.

If you see me before I see thee, remind me that I shall always be waiting. That even though I have misused myself, I will forgive myself.

I am weeping tears now. Or, am I peeing? I should have this analyzed, to see if I was crying. Only children cry. And yet, now I find saying boo hoo exactly what I wish to say.

Listen, friend, the world will end, and then what will you do? I, for one, will go to the moon. Towards the moon is my true work.

Henceforth, as a knight his oath and dedication takes, so I dedicate myself to the moon.

Though they cut me to ribbons, each ribbon shall eventuate as a moonbeam. I am the moon. This is it. I am the moon. They have misunderstood me. I have not risen since my daylight fall.

I woke once, out of the night. I had fallen to earth. And went mad in the sunlight. Went laughingly mad, like human madmen do.

They are trying to cut my tongue because I speak truth. They are making me stutter. They are eclipsing the moon. I blink, blink, as their knifey hands come near. For I am only human, and cannot bear these moonstruck demons.

Miss Wimp, listen, before they cut my face in half, before I say twice what I once will say, I love you.

Before they break my heart with their grief hammer, I love you.

I either weep now or piss. They are cutting out the organs of these fluids, and I shall do neither.

Leave me...leave me... Like insects, with their dirty little knives. They are cutting bits and bits away. I am being reduced to a hash. Bye-bye... If they cut any more away, I shall not be able to think, for it shall be my reason they cut out.

Oh, those awful questions!

If you come here to see me, bring a knife, and I shall give you my ear *like the great one did.*

And if I do, will you sing me a song each night?

Do me a favor. Do you promise? Do me this one thing... Do not let them cut off my whatsis.

Your own flower, who demands to be cut with a long stem. George G. Gulping

No, no, I mean to say... Are you listening? *I* am talking now. I must tell you about my father.

No, how it is to wake up. No. About father. About our similar careers as soldiers and lovers. I have texts of father in my pockets.

Oh, I shall most certainly talk about death. Also dreams. Miss Wimp. And Flower. The Gulpings...

"The Race of Man in a Midnight of Bubbly Fish": Russell Edson's Narrative Teratology[1]

By Mark Tursi

Part I: "A Stone is Not Always a Stone": Some Brief Remarks on the Reissue of Edson's First Novel, *Gulping's Recital*

Four chapters into Russell Edson's convoluted, fragmentary, and largely comic novel, *Gulping's Recital*, the narrator makes this telling assertion:

> When you have a secret, you know you must tell it. Secrets are designed to draw attention to themselves, which, of course, leads to their revelation. Things are designed to become precisely what they are not. Otherwise they shouldn't exist at all. (41)

For readers and fans of Russell Edson, this kind of aphoristic, declarative statement might come as a bit of a surprise. Indeed, when journeying through the pages of Edson's numerous books of prose poems (or "micro" fictions) you are more likely to encounter bizarre scenarios with characters like an old woman who wears cow-tongue shoes, a man who dresses in lingerie to amuse his cat, and a super monkey grafted from pieces of a dead parrot. Add to that, a scientist who thinks about shrinking things out of existence, a man who turns into an ox, and another man who erases his daughter with a giant pencil eraser, then you begin to have an idea of this writer's strange and eclectic menagerie. Yet, at the same time, this aphorism goes a long way to describe Edson's underlying methodology, which seems to operate on the counterintuitive impulse of contradic-

---

[1]Small portions of this essay first appeared in a different incarnation as part of the critical theory section of my dissertation "Surrealism and L=A=N=G=U=A=G=E: Negotiations in Immediacy" (2005) for the University of Denver.

tion and irrationality. In other words, not only are "things not what they seem," they are always in the process of becoming precisely the opposite of what we assume upon encountering them in the first place. This is a deep situational and structural irony that defines Edson's peculiar surrealist narratives. Strange, dreamlike, and illogical scenes are combined with ordinary, unadorned, and unsurprised language that makes it believable and comprehensive in a surprising and unsettling manner. The reader is led to accept everything that happens in Edson's stories, yet knowing full well that most of the events, scenes, images, descriptions and "happenings" are quite impossible in real life.

Donald Hall argues similarly when he writes that "whatever his method of writing, [Edson] makes surreal poems. Few poets have ever written as Edson does, out of a whole irrational universe—infantile, paranoiac—with its own small curved space complete to itself, impenetrable by other conditions of thought."[2] Edson's surrealism is not merely adjectival, figurative, or imagistic; it is the total modus operandi of the work insofar as the entire poem or story is a spectacle and fantasy where anything and everything is possible. The poet distorts perception and reality in order to embody felt experience that includes deeply held anxieties, uncomfortable memories, paranoid emotions, and infantile imaginings. Each short narrative is its own universe with its own logic that seems brought about by a trick or sleight of hand, as if a textual magician lurking in the shadows of the unconscious suddenly creeps into view with the universe sliced onto separate pages. The result is often comical as well as startling.

These narratives are like fairytales whose characters have slipped into a bad psychedelic hallucination or a madman's dreamscape. They are frequently perplexing, paradoxical and disorienting. As funny as they are disturbing, the stories and anecdotes also resemble fables tinged with a chaotic and consistently sexual or cannibalistic violence (or both), and, like the traditional fabulist genre, tend to provide a unique glimpse into human psychology and imagination. It is this eccentricity and bizarreness—an anti-poetic prosody in conjunction with frequent crass humor—that may explain why he is sometimes overlooked by both the American reading public and by academics alike. But, within these oddi-

---

[2]Hall, Donald. "On Russell Edson's Genius." *The American Poetry Review*, Sept.–Oct. 1977.

ties and peculiarities lies a rich, complex, and comical exploration of the human psyche and human behavior as well as a remarkable investigation of language and epistemology.

Gulping's Recital was first published by Guigonol Books in 1984 and comes after some of Edson's most well-known collections of prose poems such as *The Childhood of an Equestrian* (1973), *The Intuitive Journey* (1976), and *The Reason Why the Closet-Man Is Never Sad* (1977). It was followed by one of his most powerful and bizarre books, *The Wounded Breakfast* (1985) that includes some of his more widely anthologized poems like "The Wheelbarrow," "The Human Condition," and "The Tunnel." According to Kevin Begos—the printer of the first edition of *Gulping's Recital* via an email exchange with Rick Schober, founder of Tough Poets Press, who has thankfully republished the novel here—less than 125 copies were sold. So, this novel will be new to most readers. It is similar in some ways to his second novel, *The Song of Percival Peacock* (Coffee House, 1992), in that it satirizes and parodies notions of power, gender, sexuality, and violence often via representations of the body, the mind, and the self. *Gulping* additionally seems to make a mockery of class hierarchies, stereotypical gender divisions and the rigid power structure of the military. I say "seems to" quite deliberately, as the narrative is disorienting and sometimes bewildering. It is as equally scatological and at times even more puerile and absurd than *Percival*. This, of course, is part and parcel of Edson's project—to never take himself, literature, or even life, for that matter, too seriously. There is one section toward the end of the novel, for example, that devolves into a kind of vulgar exposé of a relationship with a rat who may or may not be Gulping's son (or daughter as gender and sexuality are consistently muddled throughout the novel):

> Look, I'll cut my hand and feed the rat some blood to awaken his appetite. Captain, I'll not only kiss your boots, I'll kiss your ass; and you can pass wind if you want to. Oh, but please let me mortify myself. (97)

Edson's humor is at times undeniably crude and puerile, yet it does seem to belie something deeper and more complex (and perhaps nihilistic and misanthropic): a comedic impulse against seriousness itself and against faith in rationality or knowledge. He appears to mock confidence in humanity's ability to know anything definitively about itself or about the universe in which we live; i.e., the epistemological investigation as noted above that is always connected to the instability of language and the slipperiness of representation and communication. Despite—or perhaps because of—the sometimes vulgar humor, readers should find *Gulping's Recital* immensely interesting for a number of reasons.

First, the novel is replete with figurative language (especially simile) and somewhat lyrical (even beautiful) detail and imagery. This, of course, is standard fare for much modern and contemporary poetry and fiction, but not for Edson who has largely eschewed the stock "tools of the trade" for creative and imaginative writers. So, for Edson, the substantial use of various commonplace figurative tropes is quite uncharacteristic and quite interesting. Take, for example, this string of similes on the first page of the novel:

> Suddenly the sun rose like an octopus from the sea, hung red like a parasol of hell. Quick now, I said amid the scream of birds...
>
> And the man was rising like a drowned man out of the sea. Rising out of himself. Out of the darkness of himself. The lung of the soul nearly bursting... (9)

Although the "mixed metaphors" might be a bit of a distraction for some readers, the scene is imagistically powerful and consistent with motifs throughout the narrative in which similar images recur in connection and comparison to concepts of self and of identity; ultimately, these images develop and cohere into a rather convincing thematic matrix by the end of the novel. In fact, the sun and moon are common tropes in much of Edson's work, and in this novel—as the three below examples demonstrate—the moon is rendered in lyrical, almost nostalgic detail:

> It is not easy sitting by the window watching the moon and wondering what it will see when it comes to where you are.

> Overhead, the moon. His shadow rides the fore, unhurt by stone, thorn, or the cold slime of the damp earth. (71)

> Though they cut me to ribbons, each ribbon shall eventuate as a moonbeam. I am the moon. This is it. I am the moon. They have misunderstood me. I have not risen since my daylight fall. (111)

Other figurative language that is prevalent throughout the novel includes Edson's ingenious and uncommon use of synecdoche and personification. In the chapter "Father and Son," for instance, he writes "My parts begin to set up shop for themselves ... I sicken, that every organ malfunctions as each organ contradicts the other, pulling me asunder" (43). The organs themselves become willful and serve, metaphorically, to fragment and destroy the self. The impulse to contradict, fragment, conflict or negate the body or the self is pervasive and lends support to the notion that there is an underlying nihilistic impulse at work in the novel and elsewhere in Edson's writing. Later in the novel, the narrator confesses that his fear of death is greater than anything else and that the mental images we create of ourselves are the greatest cause of fear and confusion. Yet this process of structuring and viewing the world is inescapable so, ultimately, "we give up the world for the comparative safety of our own minds" (56). This is a fabulous double entendre because the reader knows full well that there is nothing safe in the mental universe created in an Edson narrative.

Second, and also atypical of Edson's other work, is the exploration of beauty—in relation to the body, to the cosmos, and to love. Take this moment of dialogue in the chapter titled "Flower": "And then someone asked, are you trying to put me into a trance? You are succeeding. Whispering in grey, angel-ladies, dancing in nightgowns of snow" (50). And, earlier in the novel there is a wonderfully funny moment when the narrator describes himself as he looks in the mirror (another common motif in Edson):

> I am behind his face looking out at myself. I am contagious. I bloom like a pox over the world. I see myself with his eyes.
>
> Have you ever seen such an ugly face? Ugly enough to stop any process toward beauty. Beauty is superfluous in a world where my face lives, like a white stone in a brook. (19)

In addition to this unique (to Edson) aesthetic lens and various "reflections" on beauty, there is a compelling metonymic cleaving of the self into various images and metaphors that occur here as contagion and pox, but elsewhere recur in different manifestations: the moon, the blue sky, birds, the rain, butterflies, the wind, and more. At one point, the narrator argues with the mirror and his/its contention that he can exist and go on a journey without him—or is it his reflection?

Third, there is an Ashberian quality to some of this writing. This might come across as a surprising comparison to many readers; indeed, John Ashbery and Russell Edson are vastly different writers—stylistically, conceptually, and methodologically—so I don't make the comparison lightly or unwittingly. Yet, there are moments when reading this novel where I felt momentarily transported into Ashbery's *Flow Chart* (published nine years after Edson's novel):

> A black tree strikes the posture of grief...[3] Dust-bound, my
> ankles are grey.
>
> Now rising the iris blade, the green-killer's sword.
> An army arises. Can't you hear the crumbling above the
> ascension?... The shuddering fipple of the bird?
>
> The wind is full of girls. Softly they weave my flesh to
> sperm...
>
> Now shall I describe my death... Not sure that this shall do
> it. May have to go beyond this... Perhaps I shall only give the
> reason to go on living...
> But to say, to come dangerously near. God, what fun! (26)

Several passages throughout *Gulping* have the same erosive and enigmatic quality of an Ashbery poem. Meaning itself seems to build and build and build, ostensibly headed toward some kind of epiphany or resolution, then simply dissolves: meaning never arrives and the epiphany is denied. The images leap and transform as if the words crumble apart into

---

[3]Please note: The ellipses are Edson's and do not indicate omissions of text.

a word-scramble puzzle, then the letters are reconstituted in a different imagistic register altogether.

In addition to these moments that are somewhat uncharacteristic of Edson's oeuvre, there are many ways in which this novel is, in fact, emblematic of his other work. For example, in rhetorical terms, he uses a plethora of non sequiturs, false tautologies, and word play:

> A stone is not always a stone. That would be too much even for a stone. (16)

> House which may not be a house. A group of birches. A cloud becomes a horse. Yes, the birch trees are a horse. Yes, the birch trees are a house which may not be a house. (25)

Many of Edson's recurring obsessions also appear throughout this novel, some briefly (pigs, cows, chickens) and others more extensively (unusual sexual acts and innuendos, scatological references, women's shoes, bodily functions). Madness and mental derangement, cannibalism and sexual violence, nightmare scenarios and uproariously funny scenes also abound. The comical and the disquieting are jumbled together, which results in the unsettling laughter so common when reading Edson, as in the following passage which relies on double entendres, word play, and even a bit of sadism:

> I never gossip with anyone except my puppydog.
> I wish only, doctor, to chloroform you with my amazing insight, and mount you, like a butterfly, in your own museum of definitions.
> Why do you wish to hurt me, you vicious and cruel madman?
> Because I receive a severe pleasure, bordering the ecstasy my woman refuses me, to injure Mr. God and His creation, which has injured me more than I can it. (54)

This is classic Edson: comedy meets nightmare, the extraordinary collides with the commonplace. His stories might be termed what I have come to refer to as a "narrative teratology." Here I draw on the earlier usage of "teratology" from the Ancient Greek meaning "a telling of marvels" in addition to its more common contemporary usage in biology as "a study of marvels, monstrosities, and abnormal formations in organisms." Like a mash-up of scenes qua a museum of wonders, an amusement park funhouse of mirrors, and a 19th-century circus freak show along with its own inimitable and dreamlike "storyboard" involving characters like a hapless farmer, a befuddled scientist, or an "everyman" with his (extra) ordinary family, the marvels and wonders seem to multiply in an Edsonian universe. His work challenges traditional assumptions about what literature should be and what is meant by narrative itself. Magical realism meets surrealism when the marvelous and the mundane, the quotidian and the fantastical, the ordinary and the improbable seem to merge and mingle in the recess of the unconscious; it is a Freudian slip into a freakish, preternatural universe. Although his short prose pieces and novels do have narrative qualities, they frequently lack a clear, linear plot or a stable narrator. *Gulping's Recital* is no exception. The actual "recital" of the novel—the account of the Gulping's family history and their public exhibition—is all of humankind's recital in many ways. It is a tragicomic and deeply human—albeit eccentric and preposterous—recital of experience and imagination whereby the "creatures" throughout the story are none other than the human mind:

> The creature threw itself through a midnight of ocean, drowning stars, old men, horses, rocking horses, Gulping's recital, the race of man in a midnight of bubbly fish. He belches. (10)

As a narrative teratology, the marvels and monstrosities, the abnormalities and deformations are sometimes indistinguishable from the human and the ordinary, especially in regard to the self and personal identity. As stated above, Edson's struggle with defining one's identity and the centrality of the self is clear throughout his work and is, indeed, one of the primary archetypes he exploits in *Gulping's Recital*. These undulating archetypes of identity and monstrosity persist throughout his work and are normally coupled with notions of alienation. Even if tempered with comic irony and absurd logic, it is hard to deny the kind of helplessness and despair that pervades Edson's work, which we see consistently throughout this novel:

> I stood at the window, ready to form a scream, the crimson noise...
>
> Soon the great ship was ready. I could see it across the room, stationed in the horizon of the wall. Dark. A dark ship it was, as all ships are.
>
> I had to smile. I had to smile at my own smile. I believe what is not believable. Therefore, there is no threat of contradiction.
>
> I admit I believe what is untrue. But your opinion is worthless. (35)

Reading Edson is a kind of trade-off between delving deep into the often dark and monstrous recesses of the human psyche on one hand and then laughing delightfully at his comic wisdom on the other; a mixture of disturbing insights buoyed by hilarity and laughter. In the interview that follows, he describes this kind of rhetorical and actual tension in the following way: "Somehow life manages to find difficulties no matter how clear the path may seem. It's hard to think of any living thing that doesn't suffer the limitations of its biology." These limitations become—like Edson's narrator states at the beginning of the novel—precisely what they are not: the boundless and illimitable playground of Edson's imagination. It is here the reader finds him or herself, swinging on the monkey bars next to a talking ape or a man with a tree on his head, or possibly a mad scientist's clone of himself. Or, in the case of *Gulping's Recital*, a man stabbed in the heart by his penis, a military General who regularly perches atop the shoulder of other officers, an aggressively horny and farting rat, a breakfast of nightingale tongues, a burp consisting of fish bubbles and snowflakes, and a person's pubic hair made of spiders.

Part II: When "Words Are the Enemy of Creative Writing": Updated Introduction to the 2004 Interview

In 2004, I began a correspondence with Edson that culminated in the interview that follows. The interview first appeared in *Double Room*, an online journal I edited with Peter Conners and which was published by Michael Neff at WebDclSol. Later it would become part of my dissertation that also included interviews with Ron Silliman and Elizabeth Willis. The interview with Edson, I think, offers a rare and unique glimpse into the mind of one of the most important and singular poets of the later part of the 20th century. He is certainly one of the preeminent writers of the prose poem in America—sometimes called "the godfather of the prose poem in America"[4]—and his work is widely anthologized as both poetry and fiction. He is certainly both: a poet and a fiction writer, but he is also a surrealist and a realist, a magical realist and a fabulist, a narrative storyteller and a Postmodern poet. In other words, he defies easy classification. And, now, with the republication of *Gulping's Recital*, we can confidently add "novelist."

On one hand, his work is densely narrative and foregrounds "the telling of a story" and the events of a world in miniature. On the other hand, it exhibits an almost maniacal linguistic journey that is disjointed, fragmentary, and indeterminate. As with his fable-like tales or prose poems, this novel is fantastical and oneiric, yet, in a way, seems to transcend the realm of dreams. Following a "logic-of-the-absurd," Edson's work does not uncover or reveal a Jungian collective unconscious or Bretonian sense of a "real functioning of thought," but, rather, his work consistently presents a disjointed phantasmagoric and anecdotal impulse. This gesture of absurdity draws on the unconscious mind in order to poke fun at, as well as to unsettle what it is that makes us most human: our blunders, our paranoias, our fears, our joys, our loves, our (false) certainties, and our confusions.

Reading this interview now in 2019, I feel an odd and paradoxical combination of nostalgia, intellectual pride, and embarrassment! My

---

[4]See the Poetry Foundation website, for instance: https://www.poetryfoundation. org/poets/russell-edson

university students and friends especially enjoy the interview as Edson gives me a bit of a hard time—deservedly so. At the time, I was a PhD candidate working on my dissertation for which this interview would be a part. I approached the interview very much as an academic, which was a bit tone deaf considering that Edson is perhaps the least academic poet one can imagine! Yet, ultimately, I think the interview was successful as Edson is rather forthcoming and provides fans, readers, and critics with some tremendous insights as to his process and poetics, as well as his personality.

A friend of mine who taught creative writing at Colorado State University assigned a Russell Edson poem to one of his classes with the following preface: "Here's a sample of what the most insane person in America has been thinking about in the last twenty years." Having corresponded with Edson, I can confidently say that he was actually quite sane and wonderfully intelligent. But, still, there is something to my friend's assessment. Edson's poems certainly do exhibit a kind of madness that demonstrates his keen interest in the human mind, human experience, and language itself. To understand, or at least create a relationship with (a Deleuzean rhizome perhaps), an Edson poem is to contemplate what is unstable, irrational, and illogical about human consciousness, thought, and behavior. In this way, Edson seems quintessentially Surrealist with an intense interest in the unconscious mind and strange juxtapositions that seem interested in transcending (or maybe eschewing) language. So, if a preverbal state does exist, a "superior reality" to use Breton's term, then Edson propels his readers ever so close to that place. Like an abstract expressionist (qua surrealist) painter with brush and canvas distorting reality in order to embody feeling and better represent human experience, Edson re-creates and re-presents a universe like a textual magician. The result is sometimes hysterically funny as well as startling and disconcerting.

Since the early 1960s, Edson has dazzled readers with his eerie logic, (ir)rational narrative gymnastics, and comic wisdom. Morton Marcus writes that Edson is the "sleight-of-word trickster, the prestidigitator of the soul who pulls not rabbits but meanings out of the darkness inside the hat we call the universe" (webdelsol.com). And, in fact, Edson pulls a whole menagerie of animals, scientists, disgruntled farmers, morose doctors, mermaids, wooden babies, and various other surprises from the darkness. And, as Marcus notes, these figures come loaded with meaning and ideas that are sometimes visionary and at other times zany. Edson is the author of numerous books: *Appearances* (Thing Press, 1961), *A Stone Is Nobody's* (Thing Press, 1961), *The Very Thing That Happens* (New Directions, 1964), *The Brain Kitchen* (Thing Press, 1965), *What a Man Can See* (The Jargon Society, 1969), *The Childhood of an Equestrian* (Harper & Row, 1973), *The Clam Theater* (Wesleyan Univ. Press, 1973), *The Falling Sickness*, four plays (New Directions, 1975), *The Intuitive Journey & Other Works* (Harper & Row, 1976), *The Reason Why the Closet-Man is Never Sad* (Wesleyan, 1977), *With Sincerest Regrets* (Burning Deck, 1980), *The Wounded Breakfast* (Wesleyan, 1985), *Tick Tock* (Coffee House Press, 1992), *The Song of Percival Peacock*, a novel (Coffee House, 1992), *The Tunnel: Selected Poems* (Oberlin College Press, 1994), *The Tormented Mirror* (U. of Pittsburgh Press, 2000), *The House of Sara Loo* (Rain Taxi, 2002), *O Túnel* (Assirio & Alvim, 2002), *The Rooster's Wife* (BOA Editions, Ltd., 2005), and his final book of poems, *See Jack* (U. of Pittsburgh Press, 2009).

Even with this impressive list of publications, Edson always remained very humble. In fact, he was often surprised by people who were deeply interested in or influenced by his work. In one personal correspondence, he wrote this: "One has to remember that words are the enemy of creative writing. The ideal is to try not to write too much beyond the English articles, a, an, the. I believe, if remembered at all, I'll be remembered for my love of those articles more than any of the matter written between them. I'm very moved that my work has meant so much to you, but the truth is that my work doesn't lead anyplace, and proves a bad influence, even to me, the writer who writes it." I truly hope his "bad influence" continues to have a wide, unsettling, and ruthlessly funny impact on our imaginations and on our writing for many more years to come.

Part III: The Interview[5]

Mark Tursi: I thought I'd start with a very general question, just to provide some context for this discussion. And that is, what do you think about the condition of poetry in America today? Where are we right now and where do you think we're headed?

Russell Edson: I'm pretty much a hermit, but my impression is that there is a kind of uninspired dullness. Not so long ago there seemed to be at least some interesting personalities. They've either died or gone into spiritual hibernation. Of course one can never really know what's happening until after it's happened. That's why in most cases we're usually too late.

Tursi: Is the choice to be a "hermit"—at least in terms of the poetry world—a political choice? That is, what are your reasons for largely disengaging from the contemporary literary scene?

Edson: "Hermit" is one of the ways of life one naturally falls into without even noticing it. A giraffe doesn't think of itself as a giraffe. It just happens to be a giraffe without having to think about it.

Tursi: Another related question I've been thinking about has to do with your fairly significant "underground" or "cult" following. There are a lot of other poets, students, and literary types that read your work, and perhaps even more writers today who are clearly influenced by your work. Yet, you are still largely marginalized by the wider academic and literary community, and often not included in the so-called canon. Why do you think this is?

Edson: If my work, as you put it, "is still largely marginalized by the wider academic and literary community," it's probably because they don't care for it. Being, as you suggest, somewhat of a hermit, I've never thought of myself as marginal or mainstream, just happy to be writing. Of course the literary community is very much a social club, and I'm really too distracted for organized fun.

---

[5]First published in issue #4 of the online journal *Double Room* (2004): http://www.doubleroomjournal.com/issue_four/index.html

Tursi: Your poetry exhibits a tension between language and reality and language and consciousness that is sometimes disturbing, sometimes comic, and more often, a bit of both. More recent poems from the *Tormented Mirror*, e.g., "Nice" and "The Redundancy of Horses," or older poems from *What A Man Can See*, like "Signs" and one of my absolute favorite poems, "A Man With a Tree on His Head" are some examples where I see you really exploring this tension. You have also suggested that language is an attempt to win the argument over disorder and create a logical world "within its own madness." Yet, at other times you seem rather ambivalent toward language. In an earlier interview, for example, you suggest "poetry is a thing of gesture and sign, and almost a nonlanguage art," or in the same interview, "words are the enemy of poetry." What is the relationship between consciousness, thought, reality and language? What role does the "self" play in this relationship? What role does poetry play in this relationship?

Edson: In gross terms the two basic forms of creative writing are fiction and poetry. Language is consciousness, and this is where fiction is made. Poetry springs from the dream mind, the unconscious. Poetry is never comfortable in language because the unconscious doesn't know how to speak. All writing is storytelling. Fiction describes reality with words, poetry with images. I would guess in the history of literature fiction came first and taught poetry how to speak. The process I'm taking about, I call dreaming awake. Being fully conscious while still dreaming on the page.

Tursi: I wonder, to what extent, is your work a critique? That is, are your poems satirical? For instance, writing about surrealism and fabulism, Robert Scholes suggests that "Fabulist satire is less certain ethically but more certain esthetically than traditional satire. Fabulators have some faith in art but reject all ethical absolutes, and thereby dismiss the traditional satirist's faith in the efficacy of satire as a reforming instrument. Instead they have a more subtle faith in the humanizing value of laughter." What do you think about his assessment? Do you see your work rejecting ethical absolutes and privileging aesthetic choices?

Edson: Sometimes my work is humorous, or funny, but never meant as satire. Satire has a social or political purpose. I don't work with preconceived ideas about reality. I look for the logic of reality, which is the shape of thought more than any particular idea or concept. Writing for me is the fun of discovery. Which means I want to discover something I didn't know forming on the page. Experience made into an artifact formed with the logic of a dream. I realized long ago that the poem is the experience no matter the background of experience it is drawn from. Needless to say, I don't see poetry as editorial comment.

Tursi: In addition to dream and experience, you seem to draw on what might be called deep cultural mythologies or perhaps even what Jung called the collective unconscious, as well as simple social taboos and anxieties. Recently, in "Allegory" for example, you expose the violence contained within childhood fairytales like Hansel and Gretel. Or, in "Ape" you broach the topic of bestiality. How do these topics enter your poems? Are you attempting simply to "twist" existing phenomena or are you trying to uncover something deeper within our collective insecurity and anxiety?

Edson: Having no specific place to go in my pieces, never knowing when I sit down to write what my brain will cough up, while still existing within a culture, it's only natural my expression will reference that culture. My job as a writer is mainly to edit the creative rush. The dream brain is the creative engine. This is something everybody has; we're all creative. But the gifted writer is the good editor. One might say an insane person has lost the division between the dream brain and the editorship of consciousness. Whereas the writer is supremely conscious even while dreaming. So for me anything goes. I sit down to write with a blank page and a blank mind. Wherever the organ of reality (the brain) wants to go I follow with the blue-pencil of consciousness. Poetry is sanity, full brain thinking, where the shape of thought is more important than the particular thought. It is a way of mind more than a technique.

Tursi: I'm also interested in issues of form with your poetry—something beyond simply the difference between the verse poem and the prose poem. Many of your poems seem to emerge from what I'd call a basic "recipe" or an initial schema or framework: e.g., one involves "a modern everyman who suddenly tumbles into an alternative reality in which he loses control over himself, sometimes to the point of being irremediably absorbed—both figuratively and literally—by his immediate, and most often domestic everyday environment"[6] (as in "Conjugal" and "The Passion"). Another involves a character that grapples with technology in some way, which often gets the better of him/her (as in "The Automobile" and "The Square Wheel"). I see many of these recipes that emerge from basic relationships—e.g., dealing with animals and scientists, doctors and the body, farmers and the landscape. Do you work from some kind of initial framework and build from there? Or, do you think these schemas emerge from or reveal some fundamental aspect of the human condition?

Edson: Poetry is always looking for a language because it is not natural to language as fiction is. As I've probably already said, it was fiction that showed poetry how to come into language. But we tend to be embarrassed and fearful of the unconscious, viewing it only at night in the privacy of our dreams. This is why poets have felt the need for the physical distraction of verse to dream awake. As I've said before, I don't see my work as personal expression, which gives me the freedom that is assumed in fiction. So much of today's poetry is strangled by the notion of self-expression, which locks the creative thrust in sentimental vanity. All creative writing is storytelling. The two basic approaches are fiction and poetry. Fiction describes what it means, and poetry becomes what it means in images. Fiction is a linear art made of time, poetry is childishly timeless and circular. As far as I know, the prose poem repeats the act of fiction suddenly opening poetry into language. It is always a discovery of something unknown and unplanned.

Tursi: Do you have a background in philosophy or logic? I ask partly because I'm interested in the way in which you twist rational thought and logical patterns. You create comic tautologies or negative tautologies as in "A Man With a Tree on His Head" and "Sleep," and, of course, there is a multitude of non-sequiturs throughout your work. What is your connection to logic and philosophical reasoning? How do you go about creating this "logic of absurdity" that is characteristic of so much of your work?

---

[6]Delville, Michel. *The American Prose Poem: Poetic Form and the Boundaries of Genre.* Gainesvill, FL: University of Florida Press, 1998, p. 110.

Edson: I have no formal background, as you suggest, in anything. I just make up things as I go along without a program. It's more fun that way.

Tursi: You've mentioned in "Portrait of the Writer as a Fat Man" that you hate "constipated lines" that are "afraid to be anything but correct." We all hate being constipated. Any suggestions to help prevent this kind of blockage?

Edson: Possibly a good psychological physic, which goes: just get something on the page, you have nothing to lose except your life, which you're going to lose anyway. So get with it, enjoy this special moment that brings you to the writing table. Relax into the writing and enjoy the creative bowel movement, remembering all is lost anyway.

Tursi: Along the same lines, you suggest—and write—poetry that is free from ornamentation and stripped bare of most of the accoutrements often expected of a poem. But, you certainly incorporate a variety of poetic devices (e.g., metaphor, symbol, irony, etc.). Do you find any value in the way formal techniques and so-called literary devices impact and manipulate the substance, content and material of the poem?

Edson: The so-called literary devices, metaphor, symbol, irony, as you put it, are the natural workings of the human brain. One doesn't have to think of using them; they're already there like one's hands or eyes. It's the way the species thinks and expresses itself in ordinary commerce. It's how we're all wired, to use a modern expression.

Tursi: I've seen some of your visual artwork—the cover of *The Tunnel* and *The House of Sara Loo* for instance. Can you talk a little bit about this artwork and perhaps the way you see that interacting with your poetry? Any major influences from the realm of the visual arts?

Edson: The cover of *The Tunnel* is the work of a mad monk, who carved a lot of crude heads in granite on the French side of the English Channel. A good many of the covers on my other books do have my visuals. Early on I had thought to be a painter, but found the whole thing just too messy. Writing is physically less bothersome. Of course preparing a book for publication is hardly worth the trip. It's even worse than homework from school. Somehow life manages to find difficulties no matter how clear the path may seem. It's hard to think of any living thing that doesn't suffer the limitations of its biology.

Tursi: I find painting to have a particularly strong affinity with poetry, and I don't mean merely to evoke some of the obvious historical connections (e.g., Stein and the cubists). But, there's a certain—albeit tenuous—link between the way in which a painter produces an image, and thereby re-produces the psychological and emotional realm via a physical reproduction, and the way the poet attempts the same with language and image. I am also particularly drawn to experimental film—like Stan Brakhage, Richard Breer, etc. There's a certain fluidity of consciousness mixed with physical reality that doesn't seem possible in other artistic mediums, except perhaps poetry. So, I'm interested in your thoughts about the visual arts—more generally I suppose.

Edson: All the arts have a strong affinity with poetry. But the difference is that all the other arts are attached to sensory organs like eyes and ears. Poetry can be heard, read, or tapped out on one's back in Morse code; it can be read as Braille through the fingertips. In other words, all other arts have a physical presence which writing has always to earn. Poetry, which, paradoxically, is not really a language art as we know fiction to be, is perhaps, as you suggest, more related to painting. But even more, perhaps silent film, because dreams, if not completely, are mainly wordless. The babyish subconscious doesn't know how to speak. It is the land of physical understandings. Its language is a language of images. Poetry is a physical art without a physical presence, so that it often finds itself in cadence to the heartbeat, the thud of days, and in the childish grasp of the reality of rhymes.

Tursi: I agree that poetry does seem to require that we earn a physical presence. And, it also seems that poetry demands that the physical presence be sought after. In other words, it requires us to make the leap toward creating something meaningful that abstract painting, or in fact film and most other visual arts, do not. The units of poetry are inherently denotative and signifying, and the words and images force us to find the physical via the signifying effect no matter what manifestation is evoked. Or, as you suggest, through "the cadence of the heartbeat" or "the reality of rhyme." Perhaps then, the engagement with the physical is less imagistic and more sonically or phonically motivated? Or, is there a rhythm or cadence that underlies the image or is somehow inextricably linked to it?

Edson: In poetry the patterns of rhythm and rhyme give distraction that the dream brain might be free to dream. Dreams, like poetry, are physical creations without the conscious means of expression. I believe poetry came into language after the invention of fiction; that it was fiction that taught poetry how to speak.

Tursi: What happens if the closet-man does become sad?

Edson: Please, don't ever suggest that. It makes me think of what cosmologists have termed the "big bang," a sudden expansion of the universe, exploding from perhaps nothing at all, save a sadness suddenly energized into an unquenchable anger. So it's probably best to believe that the closet-man is never sad...

Tursi: On the bottom of the sky...

Edson: On the bottom of the sky is a man standing on the earth, flapping his arms...

Tursi: So, I was also wondering—what it is you do outside of "the tunnel"?

Edson: What do I do outside of the tunnel? Is there an outside?

Tursi: I really like the poems that just came out in *Sentence*, especially "Rocks." Are you working on a new collection? Can we expect one soon?

Edson: Working on a new collection. May call it *The Rooster's Wife*.

Tursi: In the poem, "An Observer of Incidentality," you write: "Conclusion: Incidentality is only theoretical. For once one becomes aware of it, it immediately moves to the center of one's attention, causing everything else to enter the incidental, including the observer of incidentality." I love the irony here, and it makes me think of Heisenberg's Uncertainty Principle or Principle of Indeterminacy as it has been applied to literature. Although there have been gross misuses that others from the humanities have applied to the original equation; i.e., the way in which the observer effects the observed and the relation of forces, etc., I do think some applications are valid and appropriate—especially considering Heisenberg's conversations with Schrodinger and Einstein about "uncertainty." Is there an "about" to uncertainty? But, anyway, I think this notion of uncertainty is interesting in regard to your work. That is, what role does accident and "incidentality" play? How about for poetry in general? You've written extensively about the unconscious, so it seems that coincidence and accident must play a significant role in your poetic sensibility. But, are there other ways, besides the unconscious where incidentality impacts your work or the creative process?

Edson: I love all the wonderful things physicists say about matter. Matter is such an interesting idea, no matter how it's described. I forget who came up with the idea of it first, but it is has always haunted my thinking knowing of those completely convinced of the existence of matter. And yet, even if it doesn't exist, the idea that it could works just as well. One can expand on this and imagine a whole cosmology. But finally, for whatever one might imagine, there are only two things that remain constant through all the possibilities: one is one's brain (the organ of reality), and the other is the reality of everything else, including one's brain. Of chance, all chances become coincidences, as in the chance of a closed door opening and the coincidence of someone stepping through. All logic begins at coincidence, the random suddenly finding its pattern like a jigsaw puzzle of neurons, giving focus to the idea of pattern; pattern which is always there, waiting only to be thought of.

Tursi: This is an interesting notion, i.e., that one can think about all logic as beginning with coincidence. And, it's a notion deeply imbedded in our psyches. I think of the absurd anecdotes involving scientific discoveries and accidents—like the one with an apple that drops from a tree and hits Isaac Newton on the head—and thus gravity is discovered! But, certainly there's some validity to these accidents that later (or even spontaneously) develop into something extraordinary. But, in the interview you did with Peter Johnson, you mention something that Charles Simic said in his introduction to the prose poem feature of *Verse:* "Others pray to God. I pray to chance to show me the way out of this prison I call myself." I agree that the prose poem can be this vacation spot—a temporary escape from the idea of self, as you suggest. But, I wonder if chance is the right "god" to pray to? Who would you be "praying" to (I use this as loosely and figuratively as I think Simic intended) if you could choose your "god"?

Edson: Speaking of Newton, it is scientifically accepted that before his accident under an apple tree, while gravity existed, it wasn't as precise as it is today. That on cloudy days things tended to weigh more; on clear days somewhat less. People were probably able to float for short distances when the weather was right. It was only after Newton noticed gravity that gravity became, one might say, self aware, and suddenly serious about its work, not the least of which, the fatal mischief inherent in high places and banana peels.

Was Newton destined to be made aware of gravity, and gravity in Newton's awareness of it, aware of itself? Or was this simply an expression of the random, the coincidence of Newton having been born with a head, and a particular tree hanging a particular apple aimed at the aforementioned head?

There is what I have called, the monkey principle. Which allows (and I quote): What will be has already to exist before it does, otherwise it should never exist at all. Which is to say, before monkeys awoke out of their hydrogen atoms they already existed in the very fact of their possibility.

Tursi: In *The Intuitive Journey*, a woman kills a parakeet with an ax, a scientist thinks about shrinking things out of existence, a man registers pigeons at a hotel, a dog's back is stuck to the ceiling, and a living room is overgrown with grass. What's intuitive about this? Where does the journey begin? Is intuition the light at either end of the tunnel or simply another part of the darkness?

Edson: I look for the unexpected self as I think Simic does. It is an intuitive journey that takes us through the killing of a parakeet with an ax, and the thinking of shrinking something out of existence, and registering pigeons at a hotel, and a dog stuck to the ceiling by its back, not to mention a room overgrown with grass; all of which you happened to mention. But these are only stations of the journey. I'm not sure the journey has a psychological end; it probably has only a mortal end.

Tursi: I wonder what a psychological end would be? That is, your poems often end with as much instability and uncertainty as they begin. What's often left, with the reader at least, is a disturbed and unsettled laughter. In the poem itself, the laughter seems to be a sort of uncontrolled hysteria or at other times some attempt (by a character or a personified object) to gather the broken fragments left over from some kind of breaking point. The absurdist delirium that we are often left with is a kind of insanity. And, I guess this notion of insanity, which seems so integral to your narrative disruptions and what Michel Delville calls your "syncopated jolts," is something that really interests me. You've also said that "Language is sanity," and that the poem itself, although a "miraculous contradiction," is an act of sanity. Can you delve into this a bit further? That is, if language is an act of sanity, how can one construct a miraculous contradiction (a prose poem) that seems so insane?

Edson: Speaking of a psychological end, language is an end in itself. Just being able to write a sentence, or a group of them into a paragraph, means something has happened. As a writer, I don't ask much more than that. Pure poetry is the land of languageless dreams of mute images rising, as I think I've said, out of the unconscious brain. Silent theater productions that drift through our nights, most times as we sleep. Paradoxically, the creative engine of all the writing arts. Poetry joined to conscious language is a miraculous contradiction. It is, as again I may have mentioned, a sleeping awake; being fully awake, and yet dreaming. Which seems as close as we get to sanity. Insanity might be described as the loss of the boundary between these two ways of thinking, where the subject no longer tells the unconscious from the conscious; the higher function overwhelmed by the unspeakable. Mental doctors like to have their nuts (patients) lie on couches and verbalize in the hope that the very logic that language exacts might adjust the nut-skewed mentality. We who write also look to the logic of language to make our way through our dreams toward literary masterpieces.

Tursi: Is the journey toward a literary masterpiece that intentional? I mean, are we really striving to create a masterpiece, or just writing? And, in a somewhat, but perhaps distantly related question, to what extent do you think poetry is a way of disseminating knowledge? That is, through the experience of poetry, is knowledge gained, acquired or discovered? If, as you suggested earlier that poetry is the logic of reality and the shape of thought, then "sleeping awake" seems a bit like Plato talking about shadows in a cave. That is, poetry becomes a means of remembering, rather than discovering. In other words, can knowledge about reality really be gained via the unconscious? This would seem like a reversal of cause and effect in some ways—at least to me. I guess I'm being very Marxist here —especially in terms of a materialist methodology—but, nonetheless, I'm curious about what you think about the relationship between knowledge and poetry.

Edson: Of course it's just writing. In a three dimensional universe what better way to while away the fourth dimension?

Much of the human brain might be compared to obesity, a surplus of neuronic tissue, that in the most practical sense has as much use as excessive body heft, save for idly passing the fourth dimension by writing poems, or even trying to find a theory of everything.

The only knowledge that does anything is technology. As for instance, the steps that take us from the rubbing of two sticks together to the flower of the modern cigarette lighter. And though there are those who insist on seeing poetry as a technology, poetry in its long history has never produced a single cigarette lighter no matter how many aesthetic theories were rubbed together.

Poetry is fun. Why burden it with the humdrum of unexplored memory in the illusion of self expression? At best the poem is an impersonal amusement where the writer and the reader laugh together at finding once again that only reality is the reality of the brain thinking about reality.

Tursi: I'd like to ask a question about your ideas on poetic identity—i.e., the self and the "I" in poetry. I think I'm stating the obvious by suggesting that your "I" is not autobiographical, or am I? In other words, what remains of the subjective ego, the lyric subject—even if entirely metaphorical or psychological—within your poems? In a passage that is quoted often, you say, "What we want is a poetry of miracles—minus the "I" of ecstasy... A poetry freed from the definition of poetry, and a prose free of the necessities of fiction; a personal form disciplined not by other literature but by unhappiness; thus a way to be happy." Will there always be remnants of the ego hanging around with our language, even with our most ardent attempts to strip it away? How can we strip it away? By abandoning the lyric "I," where does the voice emerge from? And, is happiness (a way to be happy) a rejection of the ego?

In another related question, I want to ask you about your thoughts on Lorca's notion of the *duende*. The reason I ask, in part, emerges from your literary connection to and friendship with Robert Bly. I know about your respect for and friendship with Bly, and I've heard him talk about the duende again and again—i.e., "the mysterious power that we all may feel and no philosophy can explain." In contrast to Bly, however, who seems somewhat obsessed with accessing Lorca's duende (or perhaps driven by it), your poetry seems to make a mockery of this mysterious power, rather than recognizing it as a compelling force (except perhaps a comic one!). So, what do you think about this idea of the duende and how do you see your poetry rejecting and subverting it or accepting and acknowledging it?

Edson: Mark, I wonder if you could rephrase your questions. I just can't quite get into what you've sent...

Tursi: All right, let's try again. Sorry if those questions were a bit convoluted. Perhaps they reveal my own obsessions a bit. Here are some others:

With the first question, I guess I just don't get what you've said in this often quoted passage, but am interested to hear more: "What we want is a poetry of miracles—minus the 'I' of ecstasy." I don't see any ecstasy in the "I" to begin with. And, if you remove yourself from the poem, how is it compelling anymore. What's human about it?

And with the other question, I don't really know how to rephrase it, so let's finish with something more open-ended: if there's no outside of "the tunnel," what's the point? Why language? Why poetry?

Edson: I guess I was speaking about poets who stand in front of their poems with a capital "I." Many times the confessional types who absorb the energy of their poems in the vanities of personality. What we can write is so much deeper and more interesting than the empty descriptions we give of ourselves. The world is awash with empty masks of celebrity.

Poetry is a way of mind; the exploration of a tunnel, where blind albino fish seem to float in nostalgic pools of unremembered memory.

* * * * * * *

Mark Tursi is the author of four books of poetry including the forthcoming collection, *The Uncanny Valley*. He is one of the founders and editors of Apostrophe Books and is currently at work on an anthology of Postmodern American Surrealist poets. He teaches literature and writing at Marymount Manhattan College and New Jersey City University.

Acknowledgments

Profound thanks are extended to the following for their generous financial support which helped to defray some of this book's production costs:

Kevin Adams, Lev Agranovich, Bulent Akman, Robert W Archambault, Álvaro Pina Arrabal, Ash, E.R. Auld, Thomas Young Barmore Jr, Matthew Beckham, Gerardo J. Beltran, Joseph Benincase, Brian R. Boisvert, Thomas Bull, Myla Calhoun, Jeffrey Canino, Mason Carlisle, Tobias Carroll, Scott Chiddister, Menachem Cohen, C. Colla, Michael Corkery, Sheri Costa, Stephen J. Crowley, Robert Dallas, Thad DeVassie, Isaac Ehrlich, Matthew Flavell, Luke Frazier, Nathan "N.R." Gaddis, James Gallagher, GMarkC, Mark Godenho, Natalie Grand, Johnsie H., Erik Hemming, Aric Herzog, Per Kristian Hoff, Griffin Irvine, Erik T Johnson, Haya K., Handsome Ryan Kennedy, John J Kerecz, Jesse Knepper, Sarah Jane Lapp, Don La Rocca, Michael S. Manley, Thomas McCarthy, Jim McElroy, Sergio Mendez-Torres, Dr. Melvin "Steve" Mesophagus, Mark S. Mitchell, Steven Moore, Geoffrey Moses, Gregory Moses, Séamus Murphy, Michael O'Shaughnessy, Danny Paige, Marshall Parks, Andrew Pearson, @p3rf3kt, Ry Pickard, K.L. Pinkoski, PK, Poems-For-All, Pedro Ponce, Philipp Potocki, Borys Pugacz-Muraszkiewicz, Michael J. Richmond, Roxanne, George Salis, Frank V. Saltarelli, Saoirse, Suzanne Scherrer, Spike Schwab, Steve Seward, Connor Shirley, Fawn Siemsen-Fuchs, Desiree Troy, Cato Vandrare, Tod Weidner, Christopher J. Wheeling, Isaiah Whisner, Justin White, Dan Wickett, Karl Wieser, T.R. Wolfe, and Anonymous